CALDERWOOD COVE

Also by Sharon L. Dean

The Deborah Strong Mysteries:
The Barn
The Wicked Bible

Other novels:

Tour de Trace
Death of the Keynote Speaker
Cemetery Wine
Leaving Freedom

CALDERWOOD COVE

A DEBORAH STRONG MYSTERY

SHARON L. DEAN

Encircle Publications
Farmington, Maine U.S.A.

Editor: Cynthia Brackett-Vincent

Cover design by Christopher Wait
Cover photograph by Sharon L. Dean

Published by:

Encircle Publications
PO Box 187
Farmington, ME 04938

info@encirclepub.com
http://encirclepub.com

For my friends who gather in Maine

CHAPTER 1

I BRAKED AT a mailbox that announced "The Calderwoods" above a painting of a coat-of arms. In high school Brenda painted constantly and I guessed she'd been the one who painted the Calderwood crest on her mailbox. I studied it when I got out of my car. A helmet with the visor down, three white stars on a band of blue, everything bordered with blue scrolls. Beneath the band, a red X looked threatening.

I shivered in the wind blowing off the Atlantic and wished I'd worn jeans instead of shorts. Even in July the coast of Maine often cooled in the late afternoon. I couldn't see the ocean but I could smell its heavy salt. A hedge of roses bordered the area marked for cars. They were deadheaded so perfectly that the remaining blooms could have come from one of Brenda's paintings.

The three cars parked in front of the hedge next to a pickup truck told me I was the last to arrive. The black Mercedes, perfectly washed and shined, must be Brenda's. A dark blue SUV marked as a rental car would be Rachel's. The bright yellow mini-wagon with a sticker that read Brattleboro Union High School reminded me that Krista was a teacher in Vermont. My Prius's silver looked unimaginative next to the other cars, but it was economical, the most I could afford as a widowed woman on a small town librarian's salary. I'd grown attached to it the same way I'd grown attached to Shelby where we'd all been kids together.

Brenda's house was smaller than I expected, perhaps because it was dwarfed by a rambling structure across the street. Behind her house, a one-story cottage was built in the same square design and painted the same white with green shutters. A stone walkway led between the two. Its border of creeping phlox had passed their pink blooming, their green now a perfectly meandering ground cover.

When I opened the back door of my car, a voice called from the front of the house. "Deborah. Come through the back door and join us on the porch. It's cocktail hour." Brenda's voice sounded in the same low register that earned her the alto parts in Shelby High School's chorus.

"Be right there." I draped the backpack I always traveled with over my shoulder and rolled my suitcase along the stone walkway. A wheel caught, so I picked it up and carried it over the single step that led to a screened door. The interior door, painted the green of the shutters, was open.

I entered into a dining room where a table long enough for ten people was set for just the four of us. To the side of the dining room, I heard someone working in the kitchen. It smelled like bread was baking. I walked through a sitting area that connected to the dining room and dropped my suitcase at the bottom of a staircase. Another screen door led me onto an open porch surrounded with a white railing. The view in front showed an ocean choppy in the wind. A wide stairway with half-a-dozen green steps descended, rail-less, to the lawn where croquet was set up.

Brenda, Krista, and Rachel rose together as if they were in one of the choreographed performances I remembered from high school. I hugged each of them in her turn, feeling an old familiarity. Brenda Calderwood. At fifty she had the same muscular height, the same dark brown eyes, the same strawberry blond hair that looked like she didn't need to color it. When we were in junior high school and she was Brenda Peterson, my grandmother called her Sweden's Beauty. Standing next to her, Krista Greenleaf reminded me of the nicknames the high school kids gave the two of them. Mutt and Jeff, the tall and short cartoon characters. Krista was nearly a foot shorter than Brenda. In high school, Krista colored her hair so often we joked that we didn't know its real color. I half-imagined I'd find her in Calderwood Cove with green or blue or purple hair. It was still short and curly, but it was now her natural medium shade of brown with streaks of gray that made it look frosted.

I hugged Rachel last. She lingered beside me. Rachel Cummings, the only one I'd seen since we'd graduated from Shelby High School. She had the same long dark hair with blunt cut bangs and a body so thin she looked like an Egyptian painting created before the discovery of perspective. Brenda had painted a portrait of her once and titled the work *Cleopatra*. The nickname stuck.

Brenda steered me to a table set with a plate of perfectly ripe strawberries, a cheese platter, and more bottles of wine than we could drink. A vase of cut flowers was arranged next to them. "Fix yourself food and drink. There's a chair waiting for you." She pointed to a semi-circle of four Adirondack chairs cushioned with green pillows that matched the house's trim. They all faced a view of the ocean, distant on the horizon.

Rachel waited with me while I filled a plate and Brenda and Krista returned to the food and wine glasses they'd left on the low table in front of the arrangement of chairs. "There's something dead behind all Brenda's perfection," she said as she moved a strawberry so it fell off the plate.

I understood Rachel's desire to bring some sign of messy life to the table. A spilled strawberry was the kind of detail she'd look for in a painting. "Has she said why she invited us?"

"No."

"Have you told them you were in Shelby two winters ago and that we found out who killed Joseph?"

She moved a piece of cheese next to the strawberry. "Of course not. We promised, remember? All they know is that Joseph's mother died and I came back to Shelby for her funeral."

I poured myself a glass of Sancerre from a bottle with an expensive looking French label. I set the bottle back so it looked off-kilter to the hors d'oeuvre platter. "Have they been talking about the barn and what happened to Joseph?"

"Brenda brought it up. Her favorite word is 'when.' 'When I was a kid I thought that wooden cow's head near the barn's roof was real.' 'When you and Deborah found Joseph dead in the barn.' Something's odd that we're all here together. Brenda's nervous. Watch her hands. I think she has something she wants to tell us."

I'd been wondering the same thing since I received the invitation last September. A formal Save the Date invitation with a Who, Where, When that named Fourth of July, Calderwood Cove, and the three of us who'd been her friends in Shelby but who'd lost contact with each other after high school. "We've got five days. Time enough for her to say what it is."

"Three days, really. Tonight we'll be catching up on what we've been doing for the last thirty years. My flight leaves out of Portland Tuesday morning."

I wanted to tell her to change her plans. Spend some time with me in Shelby. Maybe I'd suggest it later. For now I simply followed her to the empty chairs next to Brenda and Krista.

Krista stood and straightened a pair of sunglasses with

mottled brown and gray frames that accented her hair. She pointed to a flower bed perfectly arranged among perfectly placed stones. "It's like one of Brenda's paintings. No bugs in her garden. Colors all coordinated. No flower needing to be dead-headed."

She was right. Tall pink and purple phlox bloomed next to blue delphiniums and white Shasta daisies. Zinnias and snapdragons and echinacea would keep the garden in color until the border of chrysanthemums bloomed in the fall. Hummingbirds flew around a feeder centered in the middle of the garden.

"Is the garden your design?" I asked Brenda when Rachel and I sat down.

Brenda took more than a sip of wine before she spoke. "I'm a Calderwood. We hire help. A landscape designer comes every fall and spring to keep the garden well fertilized so it will bloom from June to October. Our cook and handyman care for it all summer. They live in the cottage you saw when you drove in."

"Must be nice," said Krista.

Brenda drained her glass and poured herself more red wine. "Sit down, Krista. Remember when just before we graduated we sat around Deborah's kitchen table? We predicted our futures. How close did we come? You first, Krista."

"I was going to graduate from college then hike the Appalachian Trail before I got a job as a teacher. The teacher part came true. I teach biology in Brattleboro, Vermont."

"I remember the hiking part," said Brenda. "We teased you about living in some forest cabin. I was going to paint the sign that said Greenleaf. We all got an invitation to your wedding in some forestry place in Vermont."

"None of you came. I can recite your excuses. Brenda wrote that she was sorry but she was working in Damariscotta, Maine, and couldn't leave her job. Or her new, rich boyfriend. Rachel was in Europe studying art. Deborah was pregnant and about to give birth. How old's that child now? Twenty-five?"

My chest contracted in a familiar emptiness. "She would be. Her name was Cathy. She died."

Rachel saved me from explaining. "She was just three years old. Deborah's husband and Cathy were killed in a car accident on the Rye Beach road."

Krista reached a hand to me. "I'm so sorry. I hadn't heard that."

Her comment reminded me of how much we'd all lost contact and how odd it was that Brenda had summoned us to Calderwood Cove. The salt air of the Atlantic brought back that awful day when I'd rushed to the hospital. I left the sun that was shining through a window onto my desk for the glare of the hospital and the smell of death. "It was a long time ago. It's why I came back to Shelby. Remember the old church building we used for youth group?"

"I do," said Krista. "All the pews were taken out and we used to roller skate there."

"It's the library now. I'm the librarian. I've even gone back to the church and I help out sometimes with the youth group. Nice kids despite what you hear about today's teenagers. What about you, Krista? How are your students?"

"They're great. A lot of them are interested in medical professions after all that happened with the coronavirus."

Brenda twisted the large diamond in front of her wedding ring. Her fingernails were perfectly manicured and painted red. "You've got a wedding band, Krista, but you're still Greenleaf. How come?"

"I never wanted to go through the effort to change my name. Andy and I have two kids. One's the athletic director at Stowe High School in Vermont. The other one will be a senior at the University of Vermont in the fall." She pulled a phone out of her shirt pocket. "Andy, my husband. Logan, the athletic director. Andrea, my daughter at UVM."

We handed around the phone, the photo showing a palette of skin tones.

"He's black," said Brenda.

"Obviously." Krista took back her phone. "We married right after we graduated from UVM. He's a physical therapist in Brattleboro."

"Do you live in a cabin in the woods?" Brenda's question sounded like a taunt.

Krista reached for a case that held glasses and exchanged her mottled brown and gray rims for a pair with clear lenses and a round frame in shades of yellow. The look she varied in high school with her hair, she varied now in glasses' frames. The sun had disappeared from the porch and I felt more like we were in the woods instead of in an open area by the sea.

"Not exactly a cabin," said Krista. "But we're surrounded by woods. I never hiked the Appalachian Trail, but I get plenty of hiking in. What about the rest of you?"

"I heard the sarcasm in Rachel's voice when she said, "I'm guessing Brenda plays golf." Rachel hated golf.

"I leave that to my husband. Gerald."

"Do we get to meet him?" I wondered why Brenda had invited only three women. Why not Krista's husband to keep Gerald company? Why not ask if we had partners who would come?

Brenda drank more wine, a sip instead of a swallow this time. "He's gone."

"Gone where?" asked Krista.

Brenda lapsed into silence instead of explaining what "gone" meant. Did she plan to show off only her husband and flaunt the toney life-style she'd never had growing up in Shelby? She'd had less money than the rest of us, but she had parents who loved her.

All of us did except Rachel, whose mother died and whose father was an alcoholic.

Rachel broke the silence. "Will we get to meet the man who's given you this wonderful summer home?"

"He hates it here."

"How could he hate it?" I gestured toward the horizon. "It's gorgeous."

Brenda set down her wine glass. I noticed that her hand trembled. "Wait until you see the bathrooms. It's too primitive for him."

I stood up. "Speaking of bathrooms, I need to use one."

"Take your suitcase inside and use the upstairs bathroom. Your bedroom is the front one on the left."

I stepped inside to the living room that flowed from the dining area. I wouldn't call the house primitive. Its perfection was as studied as Brenda's gardens. Two loveseats were arranged in an angle around a coffee table that held a low vase of roses and a set of coasters designed with an etching of the Calderwood crest. Paintings were perfectly hung and a grandfather clock fit perfectly on the wall facing the staircase. Nothing was out of place.

A door stood open to a smaller sitting room. I stepped into it, hoping to see signs that it showed more than a design for a home and garden magazine. It looked more lived in, if not cozy. Bookcases lined one wall and a copy of *Wuthering Heights* lay on a table in front of a sofa with a knitted blanket folded over its back. The painting over the sofa showed a barn, the only sign that this wasn't a magazine house, but a real home. I recognized the painting as one Brenda had done in high school, the wooden cow's head we used to call Cowpie peeking from the barn's rafter. I wondered if Brenda knew what happened to that barn.

The sofa faced a television hung on a wall so no wires showed.

No windows brought light into the room. I could feel air coming through a door at the front of the house. A bedroom, the windows open. I stopped myself from going into it. Brenda deserved her privacy.

When I walked back to the staircase, voices told me that a man and a woman were in the kitchen. Probably the cook and the handyman Brenda mentioned. I heard the man say, "Tonight. After dinner." The woman said, "We'll talk about it later." The man, burly with a shock of red hair, came out of the kitchen. He saw me and nodded before he went out the back door.

I carried my suitcase up the stairs. The rooms were arranged symmetrically, two on each side of a hallway. A door at the end of the hall told me that there was an upstairs balcony that faced the ocean. Front room on the left, Brenda had said. I went into it and saw that a window looked over the balcony to the ocean in the distance. A side window showed the large house across the street. Cape Cod curtains danced in the wind blowing into the room. I closed the window against a chill that was descending.

Like everything else in the house, the perfectly square room could have served in a photo shoot for ocean living. Queen-sized bed covered with a white comforter, a small white bureau with a design of flowers painted in blues and greens, an armoire painted in the same design, an area rug also patterned with flowers, impossibly white towels hanging on a wooden rack. I set my suitcase on a bench painted like the armoire and placed my backpack next to it. I unzipped the suitcase and pulled out jeans and a rolled neck off-white sweater. I'd look as nautical as the house.

I left the bedroom door open the way all the other upstairs doors were open. The room across from mine had only a single bed. An artist's easel told me Brenda used it as a studio. The window had no curtains, so she'd have plenty of light as well as a view of the well-spaced houses, all set back from the ocean that was just visible in the distance. This was mid-coast Maine. I suspected there was no beach, only a rocky cove. I wanted to lift the cloth draped over whatever painting Brenda was working on. I'd ask later and she could show it to all of us.

The two bedrooms at the back of the house were as square as mine. Their décor was the same, except for different designs on the bureaus and armoires, one of blue seascapes, the other of boats with multi-colored sails. I felt as if I were in a house of mirrors.

At the end of the hallway, a door opened to a bathroom. I stopped to use the toilet, surprised at how small the bathroom was. There was no shower, only a sink and toilet and mirrored medicine cabinet. The mirror told me I wasn't the teenager I'd felt like when we were exchanging stories on the front porch. I had the same short hair with bangs I flipped back, but its brown was now highlighted with gray. It had curled slightly in the salt air. I looked okay, more sporty like Krista than glamorous like Rachel and Brenda. We all could have passed for thirty-five instead of fifty. I used the toilet and washed my hands, drying them on a guest towel, and started down the stairs.

A woman was laying out something in front of each of the places that had been set. I assumed she was the cook, though she wasn't the large, buxom person I stereotyped as cooks. Flat-chested and thin, her muscular arms sported tattoos, of what I couldn't tell. She wore an apron with the Calderwood crest over a T-shirt and shorts. Her ash blond hair was pulled back in a ponytail.

I approached, holding out my hand to shake hers. "I'm Deborah. Whatever you're cooking smells delicious."

She took my hand and I could see that the tattoos were of shamrocks. "Maureen. Oyster stew. What he always insists on when we have guests."

"Gerald? Will he be joining us for dinner?"

"Off to some golf tournament. But we keep his wishes. These are his idea, not Brenda's." She put a last set of salt and pepper shakers in front of a place setting.

I smiled at the four sets. All ceramic and cheap, unlike the silver and hand painted dishes. Lobster claws, whales, golf bags. The last set, death's heads, looked more ominous than amusing.

Maureen pointed to a collection of more salt and pepper shakers displayed on a hutch behind the table. "People know he likes them. They bring them as house gifts." She turned away from the table and went back into the kitchen.

I made a mental note to send some shakers to Brenda. Maybe the ones shaped like the state of New Hampshire that I'd seen when I stopped at the welcome center in Portsmouth. The case of wine I'd brought from the state liquor store in Nashua was still in my car. We'd all shared the expense so I chose good varietals. After drinking what Brenda was serving, I wasn't sure they were good enough. I was ready for another glass so I went onto the porch.

"Glad you made it back." Brenda raised her glass in a toast. "Sit. I need to go over the house rules."

"Rules? Weren't you the rule breaker in high school?" Rachel started to twist a strand of her hair in the nervous habit she'd developed after we found her boyfriend, Joseph, dead in the barn so many years ago. I touched my own hair to signal her the way I had when she returned to Shelby for his mother's funeral. She stopped twisting by refilling her wine glass.

Brenda spilled a splash of wine on her collarless blouse. It stood out like the red X on the Calderwood crest. "Gerald's a man of rules. He's like that husband in *Sleeping with the Enemy* who wants all the towels perfectly straight. He's not here so you don't have to worry. Maureen will put your rooms in order when you go home. Just be sure you leave no evidence behind that you've been here."

Krista stood up and faced us with her back to the porch railing. "Doesn't he know we're here?"

Brenda didn't answer. "The rules. There's only one shower, downstairs. Use the towels from your bedrooms. Get up when you want. Maureen will make pancakes tomorrow, but normally she doesn't cook breakfast and you'll have to help yourself to bread and bagels. First one up puts on the coffee."

I emptied the little that remained of the Sancerre into my glass. Something was badly wrong in Calderwood Cove. "Does Gerald allow guests to make their own breakfast? Or is this because we're just four women?"

Brenda stood up, her wine glass shaking in her hand. "The mosquitoes will arrive soon. Come inside and I'll explain." She looked tipsy as she went into the house and called back, "We never have overnight guests. He doesn't know you're here."

CHAPTER 2

T HE GRANDFATHER CLOCK at the foot of the stairway sounded eight, its deep gong like the warning of a fog horn. Brenda laughed when I jumped. "You always were a jittery one."

"Overactive reflexes." I let the others go ahead of me. The stairway enclosed us then spilled us one at a time into an upstairs hallway that was darkening with the setting sun. It would be full dark before we ate and well past my normal bedtime before I could try to sleep with a stomach overfull from oyster stew.

"I'll catch up," said Rachel. She went into the room behind mine that she'd been assigned for the weekend.

I wondered if Brenda had paired us off in the room arrangement the way we sometimes paired off for games of marbles in fourth grade. Rachel and I were on the left side of the hallway, Krista's bedroom and Brenda's studio on the right. We stopped at the door that led onto the balcony. I could feel the draft coming from the strengthening wind. Brenda started to open the door to the balcony then changed her mind. "Getting too cold to watch the sun set from outside. Maybe tomorrow."

Rachel joined us as we went into Brenda's studio. She'd changed into jeans and a navy blue sweater that looked as nautical as mine.

Brenda stood in front of the studio window, her hands clasped behind her back. "I can't come up here often to watch the sun set."

"I'd be here every night," said Rachel. "I'd watch how the light changes with each season."

"Still a painter's eye," said Brenda.

"Like yours." Rachel pointed to the easel. "Do we get to see that painting you're working on?"

Brenda spoke more to the window than to us, her words slurred from too much wine. "First let me explain why I invited you all. It's not really for our birthdays. I'm the only one turning fifty this year and that won't happen until December. If I make it that far."

Krista had to raise her head to look at Brenda's height. "What do you mean? Are you sick?"

Brenda mumbled something that sounded like "That might be easier." She stepped away from the window and motioned us to sit along the edge of the bed, the only piece of furniture aside from her easel and a cabinet of art supplies. She stood looking down on us, immobile except for her lips where she was working off her red lipstick. She looked determined, not angry, but authoritative, like our high school principal about to deliver an ultimatum.

She relaxed when she spoke. The wine seemed to have strengthened her now, enough that she could tell us why we were in Calderwood Cove. She no longer sounded drunk. "Gerald never goes away for more than a day or two. When he planned this golf trip last fall, I had my chance."

"Chance for what?" Krista was fidgeting next to me. I nudged her to let Brenda continue.

"To have company. To remind myself that I once had friends. When we were kids— Never mind that. It's about me and Gerald. He controls everything I do. Except for my painting." She pointed to the easel that faced the window. The cloth was still draped over it. "He thinks it's amateurish. He doesn't allow me to paint

14

in our Boston apartment even though there's a room there with a view of the Public Garden. He says the smell bothers him. In Maine, I can keep these windows open." They were closed now against the dampening air.

Rachel had started to twist her hair into a tight black cord. "You should leave him."

"How? I have no money. I don't even have a credit card."

Krista spoke like the wife and mother she was. "How do you buy groceries?"

"We have servants for that." Brenda defended her husband. "It's not like I'm a prisoner. When I'm in Boston, I walk all over the city or a car drives me to one of the museums. Gerald gives me an allowance so I can buy art supplies that I bring to Calderwood Cove. The art store in Boston is wonderful. It's where I had your invitations printed."

"Why?" I asked. If Brenda had to reach out to friends from thirty years ago, her loneliness must be unbearable.

"I'm not sure. I was facing another winter in Boston where the only people I speak to other than store clerks are the ones Gerald invites for dinner. When I was in the art store one day, I saw a woman who looked like Rachel having some invitations printed up. It was the same day I learned that Gerald would be at Hilton Head playing golf on the Fourth of July. I went back to our apartment and found all your addresses. It's not hard to do an internet search. A computer's the one thing I have in Boston that I don't have here."

Krista couldn't sit any longer. She got off the bed and put her arm around Brenda. "You should divorce him."

Brenda pushed her arm away. "I tried that once. He mocked me, asked me what I'd live on, who'd let me have an open charge account at a fancy art store, who'd pay my health insurance. He's right. He even got nicer after that. He's controlling, but he's not cruel and he likes to show me off. I guess I'm what you'd call a trophy wife. It's better in Maine. I like the guests we have for dinner more than the ones we have in Boston. I can paint. I can talk to some of the women at our beach club. I can have coffee with my neighbor across the street."

I remembered the rambling house I could see from my room. "That house is huge. Only one neighbor in it?"

"Oh, no. Nelson Sproul runs one of the oldest oyster farms in Damariscotta. Not that oyster farming's that old in Maine. He inherited it from his father in the eighties just before I married Gerald. Nelson brought me the oysters we'll be eating tonight. He's in his sixties and his mother must be close to ninety. Esther. She still plays a mean game of cribbage."

"Does she know we're here?" I asked.

"She doesn't miss anything, so she does by now. She's nosy, but also as sharp as the young math teacher she used to be. She manages the accounts for the two rentals they have. Esther's ancestors, the Bristols, used to build ships in the attached unit she had converted into an apartment. The other unit's a cottage behind the place. Tenants come in and out all summer. Nelson and Esther move back to Damariscotta in the winter to the house that belonged to the Sproul ancestors. She knows every bit of history about the area."

I studied Brenda. Only her strawberry blond hair was natural. The made-up perfection of her face reminded me of a Barbie doll. I thought again of how lonely she must be if the only friend she had was a ninety-year-old woman.

Krista lifted her head so she wasn't speaking to Brenda's chest. "Can't she help you? Maybe let you stay in Damariscotta until you figure something out?"

I got off the bed and stood between Krista and Brenda. "We'd help. You can come back to Shelby. Stay with me until you find a place of your own. Krista can drive up from Vermont. Maybe Rachel will fly up from New Orleans. We're your oldest friends."

"It doesn't matter. I'm not leaving Gerald."

Rachel stood up next to me. "He has some kind of hold on you."

Brenda gestured toward the window. "I love this place he hates. As long as we keep coming here, I'm okay."

"What about winter?" I pictured Brenda hiding in a Boston apartment, trapped by a husband she should divorce.

"Like I said. I can go anywhere I want. Gerald's not a bad man. He gives me whatever I ask for. And I get these glorious summers when I can paint all day."

Rachel pointed to the easel. "If your painting is enough, let's see this one."

Brenda walked to the easel, put her hand on the covering, and waited until we were all in front of it. She lifted the cover back.

The Calderwood crest filled the background of the painting. Instead of an X, a miniature face stared at us. The eyes and hair were dark, the nose beaked, the mouth a slash of red. Beneath the crest, black letters painted in a gothic script read *Calderwood RIP.*

Rachel was the first to speak. "The brush strokes are angry. Violent. You need to leave here before something happens."

Brenda covered the painting. "I can't leave. I've made my peace. Painting helps and he never looks at what I paint." A loud bell sounded from downstairs. Brenda's alto voice blended with the sound. "Dinner. We can't keep Maureen waiting."

The stew was rich with butter and heavy cream and loaded with freshly shucked oysters. I passed on the bread but ate the side salad and sipped at another glass of white wine. While we

17

ate, Brenda claimed that her life with Gerald had advantages. She fiddled with her death's head salt and pepper shakers as she launched into a string of "when's." "When we go to the symphony." "When we sail to Monhegan Island." "When we visited Paris." "Madrid." "Morocco." She sounded like the girl who used to dream of leaving Shelby, marrying a rich man and being showered with diamonds and love. In those days, I always noticed that the diamonds came before the love. Brenda's marriage seemed to provide enough diamonds like the one in her ring that love didn't matter.

When she finished talking about her own marriage, Brenda asked if I ever thought of remarrying.

I remembered my temptation of last fall, but spoke instead of Irwin Trombley. "There's a wonderful man in Shelby my mother would like me to marry. Unfortunately, there are no sparks for me. So no."

Brenda moved her arm around the room to show it off. "Marriage can work without sparks."

The open space of the dining room and the living room was lovely, but sterile. The paintings looked like originals, but they were all of sailboats or lighthouses or a quiet coastline. Quintessential Maine. None showed Brenda's taste, none had the passion of the brush strokes in the painting she'd shown us. Even in high school her paintings were quirky, never placid scenes like the ones here. Only the paintings I assumed Gerald had bought showed any evidence that he lived here. And the odd collection of salt and pepper shakers. I watched Brenda finger the death's head she'd used to heavily pepper her oyster stew. Her hand trembled.

I took it out of her hand. "Why so many salt and pepper shakers? Your cook told me they're Gerald's idea."

She pulled the shaker out of my hand, turned it upside

down over her empty bowl, and let some pepper escape before she pounded the shaker on the table. "It's his statement about Calderwood Cove. His mother used to insist on those little bowls of salt and pepper and tiny spoons. She had the bowls made from wood that matched this table. He hated the pretense. As soon as she died, he started collecting these. The tackier, the better."

Rachel lifted up her golf bag shaker. "I guess he has a sense of humor. Are his parents still alive?"

"His father died before I met Gerald. His mother was awful. She spent all her time preserving the Calderwood name that wasn't even in her ancestry."

I thought of the Calderwood crest on the mailbox. "It seems like Gerald likes the name."

"He likes the status. But at least he keeps me here in the summer."

Her word made her seem like a kept woman.

"Gerald sounds like a man of contradictions. Hates the house, but likes the Calderwood history."

"His father's history. He hated his mother as much as I did. We were both glad she died."

"Those are strong words," said Krista.

"They suit what she was. With her gone, I was able to think of this house as my own."

I no longer wanted to urge her to leave Gerald and live in my house.

Maureen came out of the kitchen to clear the table for dessert. I could see the shamrock tattoos moving on her muscles. She was waif thin, but strong. "Not good?" she said to Rachel, who'd barely touched her stew.

Rachel handed her the bowl. "It tasted fine, but I have trouble with oysters."

Maureen shrugged and went back into the kitchen.

"Has Maureen been any kind of friend for you?" I asked.

Brenda scoffed. "I don't mix with servants."

Maureen reappeared with a tray of strawberry shortcakes. She set one in front of each of us and went into the kitchen again. When she returned with two pots of coffee, she said, "Orange is decaf. When you're finished, put the dishes in the sink. I'll wash them in the morning."

The burly red-haired man I'd seen earlier was standing at the kitchen door waiting for her. He scowled at us and disappeared with Maureen into the kitchen.

"Is that your handyman?" I asked.

"Leroy. Her husband. I don't know where Gerald found them, but they do their jobs in a grumpy sort of way."

Something prompted me to ask, "Does Gerald trust them?"

Brenda ignored me. I poured myself a cup of regular coffee and passed the pot to Rachel, who liked hers the way I did, strong and black, even with late night caffeine. Only Krista chose the decaf.

Brenda filled her wine glass. Whatever else her marriage taught her, it had developed her capacity for drinking. After a big meal, she no longer seemed drunk. I was more likely to have a hangover than she was. "Enjoy this now because tomorrow we have leftovers," she said. "Pancakes for breakfast then a late lunch on Monhegan Island."

My stomach recoiled at the thought of more food.

Brenda finished the last bit of her shortcake. I hadn't seen evidence of any workout equipment but she must have a routine to keep her body structure solid instead of fat. "That's the plan for Sunday and Monday," she said. "I had to bribe Maureen with the night off if she made us breakfast. I thought of walking around Calderwood Island on Sunday, but it's too far and the ferry might be crowded."

Krista had eaten all her strawberries. She pushed aside her shortcake as she said, "Does your husband own an island?"

Brenda set down her empty wine glass. "Named for his family. Now it's part of the Maine Coast Heritage Trust. Gerald likes to sail there sometimes. One of the things I actually like to do with him. There are no cars on the island, no restaurants, just beaches and hiking paths. Maureen packs a picnic for us. Things like that make me realize my marriage isn't so bad."

Rachel nudged my foot under the table. She didn't believe Brenda any more than I did. She poured herself more coffee, dripping some on the uncovered table. She wiped it with one of the red and white checked napkins we were using and said, "Sorry."

"Don't worry about the table," said Brenda. "It came from an old ship."

The table's wood was gouged and deeply stained from what must have been years at sea. It screamed authentic décor. "It's an interesting table," I said.

Brenda pushed back her chair that matched the wood of the table. "Gerald doesn't like it. Cost his mother a fortune, scars and all. I'm going to bed upstairs in my studio. I'll see you all at breakfast. Monhegan Island tomorrow. Sunday we'll walk around Damariscotta and look at some of the art galleries. Maureen will fix us lobsters for dinner. We'll have dessert on the front porch and watch the fireworks."

We picked up the dishes and brought them into the kitchen. Krista carried the wine glasses. As she set them on the counter, she said, "Nothing looks like Gerald still lives here. Maybe he left her, that's why she invited us."

"Or maybe he's dead," said Rachel.

* *

My cell phone showed just after one o'clock when I fumbled for my glasses. Armed with two Advil and a Tums in my hand—the best cure for the hangover I felt starting—I found my way to the bathroom. I cupped my hand to drink water then took off my glasses to splash some on my face. The world outside the window was spinning as much as my head. The truck I'd seen when I first arrived was just pulling out of the driveway. Its headlights weren't on. Maureen or Leroy, I assumed. An odd time to be going out.

It wasn't my business, but I told myself to mention it to Brenda in the morning. I couldn't shake the notion that something was very wrong in the house. I sat for an extra minute on the toilet to let my head clear. Without putting my glasses back on, I found my way back to my room. From the side window, I saw the truck in front of the huge house across the street. Moments later, the headlights turned on and whoever was driving headed the truck away from Calderwood Cove.

CHAPTER 3

I WAS AWAKE with the sun, willing myself to stay in bed longer than five o'clock. When the grandfather clock gonged six, I got up and put on the bathrobe I'd packed. The house was quiet. I'd be the first one to shower, but the others would follow soon so we'd be ready for our eight-fifteen departure to Monhegan Island. I went into the downstairs bathroom and looked into the kitchen. Last night's dishes hadn't been washed and no coffee was brewing. I found a container with coffee beans, figured out how to use the grind and brew machine, and pressed the start button. The grinding noise was loud enough to wake the dead. It didn't matter. Maureen should arrive soon, and someone else would be up and waiting for the shower when I finished.

The bathroom was only a little bigger than the one upstairs. Everything was renovated to look historical. The toilet had a pull chain mounted to a wooden box above it, the sink was perched on a pedestal, and the cabinet on the opposite wall was painted with the ubiquitous Calderwood crest. If Gerald craved the comfort of a fancy bathroom, he didn't find it here. The shower stall had the same tan hexagon tiles as the floors.

I opened the small window beside the shower, surprised to see the pick-up truck still gone because I'd heard it again in the night. Or heard some other vehicle.

The water ran hot and strong against my skin. Brenda hadn't told us if we needed to stagger our showers to give the hot water time to recover, so I finished quickly. When I was drying off, someone tried the door handle. "I'll be right out," I said.

I put on jeans and a long-sleeved T-shirt with a Town of Shelby logo. It would remind us all of the origin of our friendship. I opened the door to find Rachel, wearing only thin pajamas with a design of musical instruments and holding an armful of clothes. "I'll be quick," she said. "I need a cup of that coffee Maureen's made. Way too much food and drink yesterday. The oysters didn't help."

"Maureen's not here. Or she wasn't. I started the coffee."

She glanced at the watch she was wearing. "Brenda said breakfast was at seven-fifteen. Maureen should be here by now."

"Something's not right. The truck's gone."

"Maybe she went for eggs or maple syrup." She went into the bathroom before I could tell her that the truck had disappeared in the middle of the night.

Four of us sat at the table working on a second pot of coffee and eating bagels we'd toasted for ourselves. When I'd told Brenda about seeing the truck leave in the night, she went to the cottage and knocked on the door. No one answered. She returned more annoyed than puzzled and refused to let us clean up last night's dessert dishes. It would serve Maureen right if she had to scour dried up shortcake.

Krista had carried our 1991 Shelby High School yearbook to Calderwood Cove. Over our substitute breakfast, we were reminiscing about different classmates and our teachers. Shelby High School students had their yearbook photos taken outside, leaning against a tree or a stonewall in the photographer's yard.

We chose epigraphs that were printed below the list of clubs and athletic teams we'd belonged to. When we wrote something in other classmates' yearbooks, we signed on our own photos.

Krista showed us all Brenda's photograph. Sitting on the stone wall behind the photographer's studio, she looked pensive but beautiful. Krista read, "'Tomorrow we will run faster, stretch out our arms farther... And one fine morning—' Fitzgerald. The inscription you wrote to me says, 'Tomorrow we'll find our green lights.' Do you remember what you meant?"

Brenda rubbed her forehead, thinking before she said, "I looked really hard to find the right quote. It's from *The Great Gatsby*. I wasn't going to be like Gatsby. I'd find wealth and love both. It wouldn't be an illusion."

Krista ran her hand over Brenda's photo. "And have you?"

Brenda sipped coffee that she'd loaded with sugar and cream. "Despite what you might think, money can buy happiness."

Rachel started to play with her hair. "Happiness is a chimera."

Brenda shot her the kind of look she'd adopted our senior year when their friendship seemed to crumble. "I told you last night. I've made my peace."

Ever our group's peacekeeper, Krista changed the subject by turning to my yearbook photo. "Deborah Madison. You have the same hairdo as thirty years ago. But no glasses. Contacts?"

"Oh, yes. I'm still blind without them." But not so blind that I couldn't identify the truck last night.

Krista pushed the yearbook across the table to me. "Read your quote."

Except for my oversized glasses, I looked okay leaning against the photographer's tree. I read what I'd chosen from Emerson. "It was high counsel that I once heard given to a young person, 'always do what you are afraid to do.'"

Krista took the book back from me. "What were you afraid of?"

I glanced at Brenda, unable to shake the feeling that she was afraid of something. "I don't know. I was excited to go to college, but my life at home was comfortable."

"You had the best parents," said Brenda.

"Are your parents are still in Shelby?" said Krista. "Mine moved to Brattleboro to be closer when my kids were little."

I nodded. "They are. I like being near them. They'll want to know how all of you are."

"Mine are in Florida," said Brenda. "In a mobile home. Gerald hates it there. When we're in Boston and have internet service, I Skype with them. That's all the contact we have. What about your parents, Rachel? You've been quiet."

The question was cruel. All of us were friends when Rachel's mother died. All of us knew that afterwards her father became an alcoholic.

Rachel wrapped both hands around her coffee cup. "They died. Let's finish with the past."

Krista took back her yearbook. "We can look at more later." As she started to close it, the book fell open to the dedication page we had created for Joseph Wheeler. She ran her hand over the page, then spoke directly to Rachel. "Joseph was your boyfriend. I remember how hard it was for you. Did anyone ever find out what happened?"

I answered quickly so no one would press Rachel to explain what we'd discovered two winters ago. "It's Shelby's only cold case."

Brenda took the yearbook from Krista and studied Joseph's photo, the only one in color in the yearbook. "He had the most amazing blue eyes. I confess, I would have tried to get him from you if he hadn't been murdered."

Rachel snapped at her. "We only know he died in the barn. He wouldn't have left me for you."

Brenda's comment explained the tension that had built between her and Rachel the summer before Joseph died.

"Shouldn't we be leaving now to get the ferry?" I wanted to recover earlier days when we were all best friends, to get onto Monhegan Island and let the trip point us forward.

"Leave your dishes on the table," said Brenda. "Maureen can clean them up. If she ever decides to come back from wherever she disappeared to. If I told Gerald, he'd be furious. Since he doesn't know you're here, I'll have to think of some other way to get her fired. I've never figured out what he likes about Maureen and Leroy. I think there's some kind of secret between them."

When she got up from the table and headed toward the stairs, she moved her cell phone from the shelf with the salt and pepper shakers and put it into a drawer. Was she afraid Gerald might track her phone if she brought it to Monhegan Island?

The old woman who lived across the street from Brenda was walking to her mailbox when we were getting into the car. She looked stooped and frail under a bathrobe that covered pajamas she was still wearing.

I waved, then asked Brenda, "Would your neighbor know anything about Maureen and Leroy? I told you I saw what I assume is their truck stop in front of her house last night."

"Esther knows everything that goes on around here. If Maureen and Leroy haven't returned when we get back, we'll invite Esther for a glass of wine."

Krista, who was sitting in the front seat next to Brenda, said, "Invite her even if they are back. She looks like my mother."

Brenda lowered her window and leaned over Krista to speak to Esther. "We're heading to Monhegan Island. Come over for a glass of wine later."

Esther put an envelope into the mailbox. "Gerald knows you have guests?"

"I'll explain later." Brenda closed her window. "We'll make Esther feel like she's part of a conspiracy. She'll like that. She doesn't like Gerald or that her son has dealings with him."

"The oyster farmer?" I didn't ask what kind of dealings.

"Yes. Nelson Sproul." Brenda pressed on the accelerator. She drove faster than she should on the narrow road. The bagel I ate for breakfast hadn't settled my stomach after yesterday's drinking and eating. I felt queasy on the curves, so I fumbled in my backpack for a Tums.

Beside me, Rachel reached out her hand for one. "I hope it's a calm crossing."

A siren behind us broke the calm that was settling between Rachel and Brenda. Brenda slowed down and pulled to the side of the road. I waited for the police car to stop and an officer to get out and write her a ticket. Instead, it continued, its tires squealing at a curve ahead of us. Before Brenda could start again, we heard more sirens. Another police car and an ambulance sped past.

"Something bad must have happened," said Krista.

Brenda pulled back onto the road. "Whatever it is, it won't bother us. Here's our turn-off to the ferry. The police are headed straight toward the Pemiquid Point Lighthouse. We'll stop there after Monhegan. Whatever it is will be cleaned up before then."

Brenda turned left just as another siren blared passed us.

The crossing to Monhegan Island promised to be as smooth as a crossing on a Maine coastal bay could be, smoother than our arrival at the ferry. We were almost denied a place even though Brenda had made a reservation. Brenda paid her fare with cash. Gerald might give her plenty of money, but apparently he didn't trust her to have her own credit card. The rest of us used our cards and listened to the ticket master complain about our late arrival.

The ferry was small and crowded. Inside, the lower deck felt claustrophobic and the upper deck was so full there were no seats and no place to stand along the side. We ended up in the prow with a dozen other tourists. An older couple held binoculars to their eyes, trying to spot seals. Two young couples huddled against each other in the chilly air. A couple with a little girl kept tight hold of her so she wouldn't lean over the edge. The child babbled on about how she'd build a fairy house on the island. She asked if she could have an ice cream cone when they finished their picnic and I thought of Cathy. The last time I saw her she was leaving with her father to get ice cream. I was glad she got the cone before they died on the curvy road that overlooked the same ocean we were floating on.

Rachel reached for my hand and squeezed. She must have been listening, too.

When the island came into view, the boat's captain launched into a history. "Monhegan Island was explored even before the Pilgrims landed in Plymouth. The Indian Samoset learned English from fishermen who frequented the shores around Monhegan. He was visiting the Wampanoag chief Massasoit when he saw the Pilgrims and greeted them by saying 'Welcome, Englishmen.' When they offered him food, he asked for beer."

The captain paused while passengers laughed at Samoset's request. I couldn't laugh. It made me remember Rachel's alcoholic father and how much Brenda had been drinking last night. The captain continued to describe how Samuel de Champlain and John Smith had also discovered the island. So had the pirates.

The little girl I'd been listening to grabbed her mother's hand when she heard this and said, "I saw a man on the boat with orange hair. Do you think he's a pirate?"

Her mother tousled her daughter's hair. "It just looked orange. Lots of people have red hair that looks orange."

The captain finished just as we were docking. He named a variety of artists who had painted on Monhegan. Edward Hopper, Rockwell Kent, Jamie Wyeth. I tried to imagine what the island would have looked like before it was filled with the people I could see walking near the dock and in the distance. Passengers poured out of the ferry ahead of us. I noticed a skinny man with hair the orange-red of Leroy's.

All along the shoreline, boulders rose out of the water declaring that this was the Maine coast. Everything was rugged and weathered. We were the last to get off.

Brenda stopped at one of the few houses along the path. "I forgot how crowded Monhegan gets on the Fourth of July. When Gerald and I were here last—" She launched into another of her reminiscences, delivering a monologue while we walked to the island's tourist center. She seemed nervous, as if she was assuring us—or herself—that she and Gerald had regular outings that they enjoyed.

"That's where we'll have lunch." She pointed not to the large inn draped in American flags but to a smaller restaurant with a railing studded with bright red geraniums. The sea air nourished flowers that surrounded all of the shingled buildings. The whole island would be as gray as the rocks and the buildings in winter, but the colors of summer were glorious.

Brenda stopped in front of a tiny building labeled "The Ropeshed" and sided, like everything, with cedar shingles. "Whatever's happening on the island gets posted here."

Signs told us to sleep at the Island Inn or try the lobster rolls at The Barnacle or visit the schoolhouse, the lighthouse, the art studios of more than a dozen artists.

Rachel pointed to a card with a painting titled Deadman's

Cove. The artist had distorted the contours of the rocks and the surrounding ocean. The brush strokes looked as violent as the ones on Brenda's paintings. The name of the artist and the number of the studio was written in black script that raged against a raging ocean. "Can we visit this studio?"

Brenda took a map out of a wooden holder and looked at it. "If we have time."

"Do you have a plan?" asked Krista, pushing back a lock of hair that was curling uncontrollably in the sea air. "I'd like to hike around."

Rachel turned in a circle to get a full view of the horizon. "I can see why artists love it here. The light would be spectacular even on a gloomy day."

If she hadn't needed to look at the map, Brenda could have been a tour guide. "We'll walk a bit, build a fairy house, see if we have time for studios before we have lunch and catch the ferry back."

"A fairy house?" said Krista.

"Little houses tourists build out of twigs and moss and bark."

"They destroy—"

Brenda interrupted. "Don't get all environmental. Follow me."

She led us along cliffs that overlooked the ocean, consulting her map as we walked. Visitors mingled among artists working at easels set up to catch a view of the ocean or a cliff or the church appearing in the distance. When we reached the tip of the island at Lobster Cove, she led us along the other side where the number of tourists had diminished. She stopped at a spot where more artists than we had seen near the ferry dock painted at easels they'd perched on rocks. The trail was rugged, but the view of the rocks showed why so many artists had chosen this spot.

Brenda looked again at the map. "This is Squeaker Cove. Map says not to go near the surf. It's dangerous."

The warning wasn't necessary. Only a mountain goat could scramble down the cliff to reach the water.

Rachel pointed to a bank of clouds in the distance. "Light's going to change. I'd love to paint it now and again late this afternoon."

"No time." If Brenda were a tour guide, she was one in a hurry to get our visit over. "We're going to Cathedral Woods to build one of those fairy houses."

We left the rocky coast and walked inland on a path where woods began to enclose us. The earth underneath was cushy, the smell of evergreen trees penetrating the salt smell of the ocean. We reached a clearing where tiny houses made of bark and twigs and moss were tucked among the trees' roots. Groups of people were scattered in an area too small for their numbers.

Brenda became more animated. "We'll build one the way we used to build little houses when we played in the woods around Krista's house."

I'd loved those woods and those days of imagining what we used to call our Pilgrim Village. Now most of the woods in the area of Shelby had been cut down for a development of cookie cutter houses. It saddened me.

Rachel knelt down and started to gather pine cones and pieces of bark. Brenda and I stooped to gather more materials in places that hadn't been cleared by other fairy house builders. The little girl who'd talked about red-headed pirates was putting moss on what passed for a fairy house. "There's my pirate."

"Shh," said her mother. "He's not a pirate."

I caught a glimpse of the red-haired man I'd seen get off the boat. He entered the clearing and quickly left. He was too emaciated to be Leroy.

Krista remained standing. "This might be enchanting, but it's an environmentalist's nightmare."

Brenda knelt next to Rachel. "There are controls. If you bring in plastic or build something too large, it gets torn down. You get caught, you get fined. There were articles in the Damariscotta paper a few years ago. A group called The Stompers kept knocking down everything. The fairy houses are allowed as long as they stay tiny, but the cairns people used to build with coastal rocks are banned."

I was surprised at how much Brenda knew about the island.

"Good for The Stompers," said Krista.

Brenda added a moss roof to a square of twigs Rachel had constructed. "When we were kids, you didn't mind. Get down and help."

Krista looked at me. "We did have fun. Nature will put everything where she wants when a good storm comes."

I looked up through the trees where the sky was clouding over. "That might be sooner than we want." The hangover headache I'd woken up with had disappeared, but another one that signaled a change in the weather was starting.

"Storm won't get this one," said Rachel. She'd embedded the structure between the protruding roots of a tree.

I knelt to help. First I spread a blanket of moss in front of a piece of bark that represented the house's door. I set four pine cones on the moss, crushed some needles, and dribbled them over the cones. "Fairy dust." I named each cone. "Brenda and Rachel, the artists. Krista the naturalist. Me."

Brenda stood up. "The townie. At least one of us keeps our hometown alive." She glanced at her watch. "Time for lunch. No time for artists' studios."

As we left the clearing, a family with three children stopped in front of the fairy house we'd built together. The children's voices formed a chorus. "Can we build a fairy house like this one?" "Do fairies really live here?" "Will someone knock it down?" Their voices ranged from wonder to foreboding.

The restaurant was crowded and noisy so we sat on the deck despite the increasing wind. Restaurants on Monhegan Island served no alcohol and I was glad I wouldn't be offered a glass of wine with the lobster roll I ordered. My headache was building and I was getting cranky. I swallowed some ibuprofen with a glass of water.

Brenda didn't object when Rachel, Krista, and I split the bill. I wondered if she had hoarded her allowance for months to pay for the weekend's food and wine, though I suspected the wine came from the well-stocked wine rack I'd noticed in an alcove in the kitchen. She'd be able to replace the bottles we drank with the ones we brought. I feared Gerald would notice the lower quality.

The return trip to New Harbor was turbulent. The ferry rolled over a rising surf and the wind blew at our backs where we stood on the front deck. No one spoke until the boat docked and we all thanked Brenda for a day that had been lovely, even though I knew Rachel was disappointed not to have visited the Deadman's Cove gallery. We could have managed if Brenda hadn't insisted on two hours for lunch.

I walked next to Brenda toward her car. "You seem to know the island well. Do you visit it often?"

"Once a year Gerald wants to sail there. Not on a busy weekend. I've never been on the ferry before."

When she unlocked her car door and we took the same spots we'd had in the morning, I remembered how much she needed to consult her map and how her narrative about The Stompers seemed right out of a newspaper. I suspected she was lying about a yearly visit.

Krista looked out the window at the darkening sky. "Do we

have time to look at the lighthouse before the storm arrives?"

Brenda started the car and headed out of the parking lot. "Don't worry about a storm. They usually pass quickly this time of year. It's not hurricane season. Remember when the tornado came through Shelby?"

"We must have been about twelve," said Krista.

I reached for Rachel's hand. The tornado hit just a week before her mother died. "I'd rather talk about the good summers. All the time we spent swimming at the lake."

Brenda monopolized our reminiscences. "Remember when we challenged Joseph and Rachel's brother to swim across the lake? What's your brother's name, Rachel? I've forgotten."

"Teddy." I answered for Rachel, pulling her hand away from her hair. We'd all been too close for Brenda to have forgotten his name.

Brenda continued with her litany. Joseph appeared at the periphery of everything she said. "When Joseph won the jump rope contest." "When we spied on Joseph and all the other boys building their fort in the woods." "When Joseph and Rachel's brother played baseball."

I was sure that Brenda intended to hurt Rachel when she said, "Remember that day you found Joseph dead in Seth Thompson's barn? I was heartbroken."

Krista glanced at Rachel and me in the back seat then said to Brenda, "Is that the entrance to the lighthouse? Something's wrong."

Brenda pulled into the entrance and was stopped by a police officer. Ahead we could see crime tape at the beginning of the path leading to the lighthouse.

The officer spoke with the cadence of a Maine accent— dropped r's and an added extra syllable. "You can't go in they-ah. Theh's been an accident."

This explained the sirens we heard in the morning. If the area was still closed, I feared there'd been more than an accident. I scanned the parking lot to see if Maureen and Leroy's truck was there. If it was, it was hidden behind something that looked like a forensics van.

Brenda turned the car around. "Esther will know what happened."

CHAPTER 4

B RENDA PULLED OFF an envelope taped to her back door. She handed it to me while she unlocked the house. "You can read it. Tell me if Maureen and Leroy have any kind of excuse for being missing this morning."

There was still no truck in the driveway. If they'd come back, they'd left again. I opened the envelope and read handwriting scratchy from age. I could barely make out the signature. "It's from Esther." I managed to read the two wobbly sentences. "'I want to meet your friends. Come to my house for...' I think it says 'strawberry-rhubarb pie.'"

"Better than staying here," Brenda said as we all stepped into the house.

The dining room table hadn't been cleared. Through the kitchen door, I could see that nothing had been cleaned up. Brenda opened the drawer where she'd left her cell phone. She punched in a number, hung up and punched in another. "There's no message to leave voice mail for either Maureen or Leroy."

She went into the kitchen and returned with a set of keys, ordering us the way she might have ordered Maureen or Leroy. "I'm going to check in the cottage. Deborah, come with me. You saw them leave. Or saw one of them leave. Krista and Rachel, start washing the dishes before we get invaded by mice."

"Aye, aye, Captain." Krista saluted and picked up a dish with the remnants of last night's strawberry shortcake.

"I hope there's no dead body in there," said Rachel, her jibe reminding me of the yellow tape at Pemiquid Light.

I'd rather be washing dishes, but I followed Brenda across the stone walkway. The increasing wind had littered it with petals falling from the roses. When he returned, Leroy would have some cleaning up to do. If he returned.

Brenda kicked a twig off the walk. "Leroy better get back here before Gerald—" She didn't finish her thought. When she inserted a key into the lock, the door opened before she turned the key. Whoever left, whenever, hadn't locked the door.

The cottage was empty of everything except furniture. Nothing hung on the walls. No magazines or books lay spread on the lobster pot that served as a coffee table. We went from the sitting room into the bedroom. The bed was stripped, the spread neatly folded at its foot. The closets and drawers were empty. Nothing was left in the bathroom, not even a roll of toilet paper.

In the kitchen, dishes sat in the drainer at the side of the sink. No food molded on the counters. Brenda opened the refrigerator. It was empty except for a box of baking soda to keep it from smelling. Despite the mess in Brenda's kitchen, Maureen and Leroy had cleaned the cottage. They hadn't left in a hurry.

"It doesn't look like they're coming back," I said.

"Gerald will be furious." She touched a number in the cell phone she was still carrying. She said nothing, just looked at her phone as if it could talk to her. "His phone's not even ringing. I wonder if mine's broken." She pressed another number, harder this time. "Esther. We'll be over in about twenty minutes. The pie sounds wonderful."

"So it's not your phone. Is Esther likely to know something

about Maureen and Leroy? It doesn't seem like they could pack up their truck and not have her notice."

"She's nosy as hell but deaf as a door nail without her hearing aids. She's the only old woman I know who sleeps through the night."

I wanted to ask her how many old women she knew. Instead, I asked if anything had been stolen from the cottage.

She looked around one more time. "Nothing in here." Outside she paused then walked to the side of the cottage. The door to a shed was ajar. She pulled it open. "The garden tools are gone. They belong to us, not to Maureen and Leroy."

"Should you call the police?"

"What for? They're easy to replace and I'm glad to be rid of those two. They always sided with Gerald. I bribed them not to tell him you visited. Maybe they took the money and ran."

I was beginning to realize how much inviting us had cost Brenda, how much she needed our friendship.

The four of us ran across the street in a driving rain and huddled on a side porch until Esther opened the door. Without the bathrobe she'd worn to the mailbox, I could see how her spine curved into a dowager's hump. A pink zip sweatshirt drooped over her shoulders and tiny breasts, ending at pants the same bright pink, the lounging suit of the aged fashionable twenty years ago. She'd tamed her gray hair into a bun. A few strands had escaped and curled along the landscape of wrinkles on her face. Behind glasses too big for her face, her eyes belied the rest of her appearance. They were green and alive.

"Come in, come in," she said, her voice stronger than her body. Her hands were small and blue-veined, but her grip was strong as she shook our hands and repeated our names. "Deborah.

Rachel. Krista." She looked at Brenda. "You said that Gerald knows they're he-ah." Only the "he-ah" marked her as a Mainer.

Brenda avoided answering. "They were my best friends back in Shelby. Still are."

We hung our wet jackets on a coat rack that stood just inside the door and followed Esther through a sitting room into a dining room where a pie looked like a centerpiece in the middle of a table, its lattice crust as perfectly woven as one from a bakery. Five places were laid out with bone china plates and tea cups in a floral pattern. The cutlery was silver, the napkins linen. Everything was set on incongruous plastic placemats. The lettering explained them. "Sproul's Oyster." I couldn't read the rest or see the logo, but I remembered Brenda telling us that Esther's son, Nelson, ran an oyster farm.

Ball-fringed curtains like the ones in Brenda's guest bedrooms moved with the wind that was blowing outside. This was a summer house, poorly insulated. Esther had built a fire in a woodstove in a corner, but I could still feel the draft.

"Nasty night," she said. "Kind that gives Maine a bad name. But I like it. Keeps the tourists away." She disappeared through a side door that led into her kitchen while we all found a chair.

Moments later, she returned carrying a tray with a teapot, lemon slices, and cream and sugar. She set the tray in front of the empty chair and sat at the head of the table, her back to the woodstove. Brenda and Krista sat closest to her, facing each other across the table. I sat next to Brenda, feeling the draft from the window. Across from me, Rachel adjusted her scarf so it blocked the draft from her neck. I regretted that I hadn't packed one for the weekend.

Esther removed a tea cozy in the design of a lobster and passed around the pot. The tea smelled heavy and black, so I added both sugar and lemon to mine, wishing she had offered coffee instead. She cut the pie into six pieces and put a generous slice onto the plates we passed to her. "Last piece is for Nelson. He's been away all day tending the oysters. Should be home soon."

Krista squeezed lemon into her tea. "Do oysters need a lot of care?"

Esther sipped tea that she drank black, nothing added to soften the taste. "It's complicated and hard work."

"Can you explain it?" Krista was interested in anything that involved nature.

Esther used the tone of an expert. "When the oysters are ready to spawn—that means have sex—they're put into containers until they release all their eggs and sperm. The fertilized eggs go into another tank and get fed filtered algae."

She stopped for a bite of pie. A line of pink juice dribbled from her mouth as she continued. "After a couple of weeks, those babies go into a floating bed to grow in sea water. The Damariscotta River and the bay are the perfect environment for producing perfect oysters. Kind of like a mother's womb."

She wiped her mouth on her linen napkin. "They get checked regularly even in winter. The whole process takes much longer than nine months. More like a couple of years."

"Does Nelson do most of the work himself?" Krista forked another piece of pie. "This pie is delicious, by the way."

Esther laughed. "He harvests over a million oysters a year. Has twenty-four employees. Boat crews, sorters, marketers. He even works with a research specialist from the University of Maine."

Krista washed down her bite of pie with a sip of tea. "Does the specialist check on environmental regulations?"

Brenda slammed down her fork. "Don't get all eco-correct. The only environmental problem with oyster farming comes from climate change."

Esther pointed her fork at Krista. "Everything in oyster farming is as natural as having a baby."

I stopped myself from educating Esther on in vitro techniques. She poured herself more black tea. "Visit Sproul's Oyster Farm tomorrow. We grow three varieties. Small and mild to medium with a hint of citrus to the largest and saltiest."

Esther spoke like she was part of the operation. Brenda had said that she kept financial records, but they must involve rental properties only. A large oyster farm would need a complicated computer program, though I shouldn't assume that Esther couldn't master one. She was old, but she was sharp. "What's happening to the oysters with climate change?" I asked.

A piece of rhubarb fell onto Esther's sweatshirt. She pinched it off and put it in her mouth. "Nelson's worried about the water warming too much and getting too acidic. That's why he works with a professor from the university."

"Seems like Maine is the perfect place for growing more than oysters. Are these strawberries and rhubarb from your garden?" Krista tried to make up for her suggestion that oyster farming hurt the environment.

Esther's wrinkles smiled. "Garden's out back. I'll show you tomorrow when the rain stops. Brenda, can you loan me Leroy to help clean up any damage the wind does?"

Brenda sat back in her chair and folded her arms. "Leroy's gone. So's Maureen."

"Gone way-ah." Esther's accent crept in, as if the mention of Leroy and Maureen made her nervous.

Brenda looked at me. "Deborah, tell Esther what you saw last night."

I set down the bite of pie I was about to put in my mouth. "I was in the bathroom and I saw their truck leaving. When I came back into my room, I saw it stopped in front of your house before someone drove it away. Much later, I heard another vehicle, but I didn't get up to see what it was."

"Why would you get up? People vacation here. They come and go at all hours. Me? I take out my hearing aids and sleep through everything." Esther sipped more tea. I wondered how she could sleep at all with that much caffeine this late at night.

When Esther set her cup down, Brenda pressed her hand. "Maureen and Leroy are gone. Not just for the night. They've taken everything. Even Gerald's tools."

"Gerald won't like that. Won't like these girlfriends of yours being here either." Esther sounded hostile, as if she disliked Gerald.

"Gerald doesn't care," Brenda lied. "You know everything that goes on around Calderwood Cove. Do you have any idea why Maureen and Leroy left?"

"Always thought they were strange ones," said Esther. "Maybe they were in witness protection or something. Part of the Irish Mafia. I remember that Whitey Bulger guy."

Brenda laughed. "Right. The Boston guy who got caught in California and murdered in prison a few years ago. I love your imagination. The mob left Boston and took up the oyster trade instead of the drug trade."

The door opened and a deep voice said, "Looks like I'm missing a party."

I turned to look at the man who spoke. He was taking off a heavy raincoat and hanging it on the coat rack. He was a small man, under five and a half feet, and wiry thin. His hair was the same gray as Esther's, curling wildly around his ears.

"Join us for pie." Esther gestured him to the table. She slipped the last piece of pie onto a plate.

He walked past us into the kitchen. "As soon as I get a beer."

When he came back into the room, he sat at the opposite end of the table from Esther. He looked about sixty and had a five o'clock shadow on his face. "And these ladies are?"

"This is my son, Nelson." She pointed at each of us. "These are Brenda's friends from way back when they were kids. Deborah. Rachel. Krista."

"Gerald know they're here?" Nelson dropped his *r*s but didn't have the heavy accent Esther sometimes had.

"Nev-ah mind that. Leroy and Maureen have flown the coop." Esther seemed to exaggerate her accent on purpose.

Nelson took off his glasses and wiped them on the linen napkin. Even in the dim light I could see that he had the same green eyes as Esther. "You mean they've left? I thought they might."

"You know something," said Brenda.

Nelson forked a large bite of pie. "Gerald found out something about them. Didn't tell me what, but he wasn't happy. I think he was going to fire them."

"He never told me anything," said Brenda.

Nelson spoke through a mouthful of pie. "Since when does he tell you anything about his business?"

Brenda clenched her fist. "Gerald doesn't have a business. Leroy and Maureen took his tools."

Nelson drank from his can of beer. "Not surprised. They were a shifty lot. Maybe they have something to do with what happened at Pemiquid Light."

"What happened at the lighthouse?" said Esther. "The radio just said it was closed for the day."

I thought of the crime tape. Maybe Maureen or Leroy was dead, the other one fled.

"Bunch of the guys were talking about it when they came in for work. Seems there might have been a murder." Nelson finished the last large bite of his pie. "Pie's good, Mum. As usual."

Esther leaned forward eagerly. "Forget the pie. A murder at the lighthouse?"

"All speculation. I just know a body was found."

"Or bodies." Like me, Brenda must have been thinking of Maureen and Leroy.

Nelson stood up. "We'll know tomorrow. Right now I'm going to bed. After this storm, it will be a tough day going out to check on the oyster beds. Guess all these ladies will be gone before Gerald gets back." He ran his green eyes over Brenda's body. "Good night for now." I cringed at the innuendo in his voice.

By ten o'clock, we were drinking wine in the sitting room where the painting of the barn hung over the sofa. I was too focused on the disappearance of Maureen and Leroy and a possible murder at Pemiquid Light to think about what had happened in the barn so long ago.

Between sips of wine, Brenda chewed on her fingernails, destroying their perfect polish. "Leroy must have murdered Maureen."

"Why would he do that?" Krista was drinking water from her wine glass. Wiser than me, she knew when to shut herself off.

Brenda stopped biting her nails. Her diamond clinked against her glass when she refilled it. "I don't know. Maybe they're both dead."

"That's crazy," said Krista. "More likely someone fell into the ocean and the body washed ashore."

"An artist probably got up early to catch the sunrise on canvas." Rachel tried to sound calm, but I knew she was nervous. She couldn't stop playing with her hair. "It would have been a perfect morning for it."

"And died how?" said Krista.

"Heart attack's most likely." Rachel's words coincided with a loud knock on the door.

"It's too late," Brenda said. "No one should be here." She carried her wine glass out of the room and went toward the back door. We all followed her.

A gust of wind slammed the screen door against the house. Brenda opened the interior door. A man wearing a rain jacket, water pouring off his hat, and a woman with the hood of her jacket covering her head stood side by side in the darkness.

The man spoke first. "Can we come in, Brenda? We have some bad news."

CHAPTER 5

"Scotty." Brenda knew the man. She looked at us. "Scotty Holland's our sheriff."

He was big, at least six feet and two-hundred-fifty pounds under a jacket that identified him as the Lincoln County Sheriff. His clean-shaven face looked younger than his body. Drops of water fell onto the doormat when he took off his hat. His hair was brown and cut short.

Brenda kept him and the woman who followed him standing just inside the door. "Is it Leroy or Maureen or both?"

"Not about them. Do you know Patsy?" He gave her no last name. She was half his size and twice his age.

Brenda glanced at the woman. "Yuh. She's a grief counselor. Why is she with you? If this has anything to do with Maureen and Leroy, I won't need a grief counselor. I didn't even like them."

"It's not about them," the sheriff repeated.

"Well, they're gone. Stole all of Gerald's tools. You knew them, Scotty. Any idea where they went?"

"You should sit down." The woman the sheriff called Patsy gestured toward the one of the loveseats in the living room.

Brenda put both hands on the wine glass she was still holding. I put my arm around her waist, led her to the loveseat, and sat down close to her. If a sheriff and a grief counselor were here in the middle of a stormy night, they were here to tell her something bad.

Patsy squeezed on Brenda's other side. Holland motioned Rachel and Krista to the other loveseat. He stood looking down on Brenda. "I'm surprised you have overnight guests, but that's good."

"Gerald knows they're here," Brenda lied. "He's in Hilton Head. Playing golf."

Patsy put her hand on Brenda's thigh, water dripping from her sleeve onto Brenda's designer jeans. "I'm sorry. We found Gerald at Pemiquid Light this morning. He's dead."

Brenda pushed Patsy's hand away, spilling some of her wine onto the water spot. "No. That's not right. Gerald's at Hilton Head."

Holland took Brenda's wine glass and set it on the coffee table in front of the loveseat. "I'm sorry. It's Gerald." There was a softness in his voice that belied his large body. "The medical examiner at the crime lab in Augusta confirmed his identity."

Brenda spoke in a register higher than her usual alto voice. "You knew Gerald. You wouldn't have sent him way off to Augusta." She used the past tense.

"It was hard to identify him," Holland said, omitting another mention of a crime lab.

"That's impossible." Brenda rubbed at the spill on her thigh. "He flew to Hilton Head. How could he be at Pemiquid Light?"

"That's what we want to find out." Holland spoke gently. "I'm afraid he was murdered."

Brenda jumped off the loveseat and said again, "That's impossible."

"We found evidence that he was stabbed before he fell into the water."

Brenda pounded on him. "Why are you lying? Gerald's in Hilton Head."

I stood up and pulled Brenda back to the loveseat. Patsy started to explain. "It's Gerald, Brenda. He—"

"Stabbed with what?" Brenda lowered her voice into a monotone. She sounded theatrical.

"We don't know yet," said Holland.

"You're wrong. I bet you found Leroy, not Gerald. He's gone. Stole Gerald's tools. Probably stole his boat, too. He knew where Gerald docked it. Maureen must have murdered her husband. How could you mistake Gerald for Leroy? Didn't you notice the red hair? Didn't he have his wallet or something in his pocket?"

Holland spoke patiently. "The hair was sandy colored and there was no wallet on the body. It was pretty banged up. The crime lab identified the fingerprints. We confirmed Gerald's dental records with Dr. Kitchell."

"Gerald wasn't a criminal." Brenda persisted in her denial. "You couldn't have found his fingerprints in some police data base."

"It doesn't matter." Holland avoided giving any details.

I knew there were all kinds of reasons that fingerprints would be on file, but I couldn't shake the feeling that there was something in Gerald's past Brenda had been holding back. All we knew was that he was controlling and wealthy. She hadn't told us where his wealth came from. Even though he hated this summer house in the cove, he seemed to value the family name. The Calderwood crest appeared all over it. Was he living on an inherited fortune or did he earn money from some job in Boston? Whether he had a criminal record or not, something was wrong. Innocent men didn't get murdered.

Holland continued to speak softly. "It would be helpful to know how he was going to Hilton Head."

Brenda still spoke in a theatrical monotone. "He flew out of Portland at some god-awful hour on Thursday. Ask Nelson Sproul. He drove him to the airport."

"We'll check on that," said Holland. "We need to find his boat. It's not at its mooring."

Brenda jumped off the loveseat again. She stood rigid, staring out the window that overlooked the front porch. "The yard will be a mess tomorrow. Leroy will have a lot of work to do."

Rachel, Krista, and I all went over to her. Rain swirled outside in the wind. "Leroy's gone," said Krista. "We'll help you clean up the yard."

Brenda looked down on her. "Gerald doesn't let me do yard work." She turned toward Holland. "You'd better find them."

"Them?" Patsy said in the soft voice of someone paid to be a comforter.

"Leroy and Maureen. They're crooks." Brenda faced the window again.

We stepped away to let Holland and Patsy stand where they could talk with her.

"I saw Leroy last week," said Holland. "He was buying a mini-safe. For important papers, he said, in case of a hurricane. The O'Donnells have lived here winter and summer for how long? Three years, maybe? Odd that he'd only be getting around to buying a safe now. Any idea what was so important?"

"Just find them," said Brenda. "Gerald will be furious."

Patsy spoke softly again. "Gerald's dead."

Brenda snapped at her. "I know that. I'm not crazy with grief. Just find the O'Donnells. I'll have to hire another gardener, but I want those tools back."

"We'll look into it. We'll want an inventory."

"What difference does it make? Just find them." I couldn't tell if Brenda meant the tools or the O'Donnells.

"Any idea where Gerald found Leroy and Maureen?" said Holland. "Maybe through an agency?"

Brenda moved away from the window. "I have no idea. They

just appeared one day. Go do your jobs. I'm going to bed." She grabbed her glass and went into the sitting room where we'd been drinking wine. Moments later she came back with it full. "You can leave now."

"I can stay the night," said Patsy. "It will be a hard one."

"Not that hard." Brenda took more than a sip of wine. "My friends are here. We'll be fine."

"We'll have questions for you in the morning." Holland chose his words carefully. "Someone will take you to Berkinshaw's. You'll need to make arrangements for Gerald."

"Burn him." Brenda walked alone up the staircase.

I saw Holland and Patsy to the door. Patsy looked toward Rachel and Krista, who were talking at the window, their backs to us. "Take turns sitting up with her tonight."

Holland put on his hat and opened the door. As they stepped into the storm, I heard Patsy say, "I'm surprised Gerald let her have guests."

I could just hear Holland say, "That's enough. Their relationship is none of our business."

I joined Rachel and Krista at the window. Rachel was working furiously to twist strands of her hair into a cord. I feared Gerald's murder had triggered memories of Joseph. I moved her hand away from her hair and said, "This is different."

"What do you mean different?" said Krista.

"We've both lost people we love. It doesn't seem that Brenda loved her husband." I remembered the hollow feeling, the pain that came into the pit of my stomach along with the tears when I learned that Nathan and Cathy had been killed. My neighbor sat with me all day and all night while I alternately slept and woke, reaching for Nathan or hearing Cathy's cries before the numbness descended and I remembered what happened.

As we turned away from the window and the storm that

raged against the night, Krista said what we were all thinking. "Something's wrong. One minute Brenda denies that her husband is dead, the next she doesn't seem to care."

We found Brenda in front of the easel that faced the window, the painting of the miniature face against the Calderwood crest thrown on the floor. Brenda stepped on it. "Join me. Like The Stompers on Monhegan."

She stomped once on the face then returned to her easel. Whatever she planned to paint, she'd switched from the oils and heavy canvas of the Calderwood painting to watercolor paper. She'd tilted her easel, but it wasn't flat enough to keep watercolors from dripping. She was using light colors, yellow and pink and pale turquoise. Her brush strokes were soft, not angry like the ones on the oil painting. She added a dab of peach that bled into a line of yellow. It wasn't the storm that she painted.

"Maybe you should wait until morning," said Rachel. "The storm will be over and you can capture the sunrise."

"The sunrise is in my head." Brenda put the brush in a jar of water and picked up the glass of wine she'd set next to the palette of watercolors. When she sipped, she added more lipstick to what was already on the rim of the glass. "I'm not surprised he's dead."

Krista looked shocked. "Not surprised he was murdered?"

Brenda drained her wine. "I suspected a few years ago that he was involved in something illegal."

"Why would you think that?" I said.

Brenda exchanged the wine glass for a small paint brush. She added a splotch of turquoise to her painting. "The O'Donnells. We always hired locals at Calderwood Cove. Gerald used the cottage as an office. When he hired Maureen and Leroy, he didn't need an office anymore because he stopped working."

Krista moved Brenda's wine glass so it wouldn't fall off the table. "What kind of work?"

Brenda ignored her and dipped the paint brush into the water and wiped it on a painter's cloth. She studied the few lines she'd painted.

"What kind of work?" Krista asked again.

"He was an accountant. He knows—knew—how to manipulate money."

"Why didn't you go to the police?" I feared Gerald had controlled Brenda in ways beyond her pocketbook.

Brenda added a line of pink to her painting. The line ran down the paper. It reminded me of the pie juice running down Esther's chin. "Why would I? I don't care how Gerald made his money. It's all mine now."

Rachel reached for Brenda's paint brush. "You can paint in the morning."

Brenda swiped it across Rachel's bangs. "Now you look like Cleopatra with a pink headband. Wonder how Joseph would have liked the effect."

Krista took the brush away from Brenda and led her to the bed. "You should get some sleep." She pulled down the covers and tucked her in.

We waited, silent. I remembered our slumber parties as kids. Brenda would fall asleep mid-sentence. After Rachel, Krista, and I stopped talking, I would lie awake listening to breathing. I was always the last to fall asleep.

A limb crashed at the side of the house near the flower garden. I jumped. Brenda didn't stir at the sound. She slept as deeply as she did when we were kids.

We left the room together. Krista brushed Rachel's bangs. "That was cruel."

"Don't worry about it. Watercolors will wash out." Rachel went into her room.

"When I agreed to this reunion, I was remembering our early days," said Krista. "I'd forgotten that Brenda and Rachel barely spoke during senior year."

"Rachel was suffering. She barely spoke to any of us. Brenda will calm down in the morning." I went into my room and stood in front of the window until I heard first Krista, then Rachel, finish in the bathroom. The wind that had downed the tree limb was the storm's last gasp. I could see the rain decreasing from a downpour slanting across the night to a steady falling. Across the street, the Sproul's house rose in the darkness like some ghost ship that had been built there. Esther kept the financial records. Gerald had been an accountant. The connection felt like a blast of wind. I pushed it away and took my turn in the bathroom.

I woke needing to use the toilet. Black tea was worse on my bladder than black coffee. The house was cold, so I put on my robe before I found my way to the bathroom. A door slammed outside. I looked out the window, thinking the wind had caught the screen to the cottage. The rain had stopped and the trees had quieted. The motion detector at the side of the main house flashed on, then off. Without my contact lenses, I could see nothing that triggered it. Skunk hour, I told myself.

Rachel was standing at the bathroom door when I came out. "My turn. Then come talk for a minute. She motioned me toward her bedroom. Minutes later, we were sitting on her bed, our backs against the headboard, our knees comfortably bent, the way we'd exchanged confidences so many times when we were in junior high.

I pulled the spread over my knees. "Are you thinking about Joseph?"

"I'm okay. I made my peace when we found out what happened to him."

"You sound like Brenda. She made her peace with a crappy marriage." I focused my eyes on the pattern of the bedspread instead of the blurry contours of the room. "She was faking in front of the sheriff. She knew Gerald was involved in something illegal."

Rachel said what I'd been thinking. "She knew right away that Gerald was dead. Why didn't she cry?"

"She basically told us. She's free of him and she'll have money of her own."

Rachel pulled her knees tight against her chest. "She has expensive tastes. That easel she uses costs over five hundred dollars. I think she killed Gerald."

"How could she have done that? And when?"

She twisted around her knees so she could see out the window. "Before we arrived. There's something funny about Nelson Sproul. Maybe he did it for her."

I pulled the spread higher so it covered both of us. "Next you'll be accusing Esther."

"Don't be silly. She's too old to get a dead body into a boat and capsize it at sea."

"We don't know where the boat is."

Rachel kicked off the spread and stretched her legs out. "Nelson then. His motive?"

"Esther keeps the financial records, I assume for the rental properties, not the oyster farm. Gerald quit his job as an accountant. Maybe he was using the oyster farm to launder money. The sheriff didn't say what was used to stab him. Maybe it was something connected to oyster farming."

"He could have teamed up with the O'Donnells. The weapon might be one of the tools they stole. There's a reason they disappeared in the dead of night."

I swung my legs to the side of the bed and stood up. "This one's not for us to investigate. Get some sleep. Brenda will need us in the morning."

"Need you. She's never needed me." Rachel lay under the covers.

I went back to my room. A sliver of moon had appeared from behind the clouds. Its arc pointed to the Sproul house like an accusing finger.

CHAPTER 6

I woke with the knowledge of Gerald's murder slowly coming into my consciousness. I thought of leaving a note, driving home, getting away from Brenda's odd reaction to the death of her husband. Grief didn't seem like the appropriate word. Maybe shock, or denial, or fear. Even relief. Rachel would add guilt. I wasn't ready to think that.

I kicked off the covers and got out of bed to see what damage the storm had done. Without my contact lenses, I could see only the blur of the sunrise in an impressionist painting, lovely but as indistinct as Brenda's reactions. I found the glasses I used at night and could just make out two figures looking like blobs of black paint in front of the apartment that rose like a ship that had once been built there. One of the blobs moved into the apartment, the other to the low shape of a truck. Nelson Sproul must have spoken with his renter before leaving for the oyster farm.

I heard Brenda in her room, so I stepped across the hall to check on her. She was painting. Her hair fell, uncombed, against her silk nightgown. Its reddish tint blended with the nightgown's patterns of mauve and pink swirls. She spoke before I did, her voice groggy from sleep. "The sunrise woke me. I had to paint it. You should go back to sleep."

"I'm awake now. Can I sit with you?"

"You don't need to." She replaced one brush with another and continued painting. "When the sun woke me and I remembered what happened, I felt freer than I have in years. Is that awful?"

"Honest, not awful." My urge to leave disappeared as Brenda acknowledged her feelings. She would need our support for the next few days.

She stopped painting and looked at me. "I'm sure I'll miss him. He took me to nice places. We had the best seats to any play I wanted to see and I like the guests he invited when we're in Maine. It helped that he was good in bed."

I remembered in high school when Brenda told us she'd lost her virginity. With the guy we called Paul the Pole. He'd been a friend of Joseph Wheeler's. Krista and I talked about how Brenda was using Paul as a substitute for Joseph. Naive teenagers, we had a long discussion about sex without love. Apparently that wasn't a problem for Brenda.

"You were married for a long time," I said. "Grief will creep up on you. Maybe you should try to sleep again. The sheriff will be back with more information and loads of questions. You'll need to tell him that you thought Gerald was involved in something illegal."

"I shouldn't have told you that. Promise me you won't say anything."

I wanted to challenge her, to tell her that the police needed to know so they could find Gerald's killer. "They'll find out sooner or later."

She turned to her painting. "Go back to bed. I hadn't realized how much I'd accepted the life Gerald gave me. Let me at least enjoy my freedom for a few hours."

I understood what she meant. There were moments after Nathan and Cathy died when I felt lighter. I had no one to worry about except myself. Then I would lie in bed alone and cry for the clutter of Cathy's toys, Nathan's shirts that took up too much of the closet, the magazines he left in every corner of the house. Cold seeped from my bare feet into my whole body. I went back to my room, crawled under the covers, and wept in a way I hadn't in years.

The air smelled fresh and salty. The damp of the night's rain rose in a mist from the grass. Rachel had started to pile sticks in a trash barrel the O'Donnells had left in the tool shed. We needed rakes so I crossed the street to borrow some from Esther. She answered the door before I knocked. Her hair was tied neatly in a bun and she'd exchanged her pink lounge suit for a yellow one, a spill of tea darkening the front.

She greeted me with a question. "What was Scotty Holland doing at Brenda's last night? I saw his sheriff's car when I was brushing my hair. I went into Nelson's room and told him he should go over there. He was on the phone with someone. Just said I'd find out in the morning and went back to talking."

"Do you know who he was talking to?" I couldn't shake my suspicion that Nelson knew something about the O'Donnells and that there was some connection to Gerald's murder.

Esther stepped onto the porch. She avoided answering my question. "Poor Nelson. Oysters don't stop needing attention even on the Fourth of July. It'll be hard going today after the storm. The sheriff? Were they asking about the O'Donnells?"

I wasn't ready to tell Esther that Gerald was dead. She'd find out soon enough. "Something like that. Do you have a couple of rakes we can borrow? We're cleaning up Brenda's yard."

From behind her glasses, Esther fixed her green eyes on me. She knew I was holding back. "Bet Gerald doesn't know Brenda has company. He's a controlling one. Won't even let her join the Cove cribbage group. He says all they do is chit chat. Can't understand why Nelson bothers with him."

"Do he and Gerald often talk? Maybe he knows why the O'Donnells left."

"Nelson doesn't tell me anything. But he leaves things hanging around. Come inside. We can look through his papers. Can't figure out that computer he has, but maybe you can. What do you need? A passcode or something?" Esther was too eager. If she didn't know something about Nelson and the O'Donnells, she suspected something. I wanted to know what.

"I'll come back after I get the rakes. Do you have more than one?"

"Follow me." She stepped out of her slippers and walked barefoot around the side of the house. Water that lingered on the grass soaked through my sneakers as I followed.

I started toward a shed I saw behind the house, but Esther stopped me. "Not there." She led me to a door in back of the attached barn and pointed to a sign that hung next to it. The sign showed the faded outline of some kind of sailing ship and words, equally faded, that read *Bristol's Shipbuilding*. "My ancestors used to build ships here." She spoke with the kind of pride Gerald displayed in all his Calderwood crest designs.

The man I must have seen earlier appeared. He was young, maybe in his twenties. Running shorts and a T-shirt showed off long legs and muscular arms. His sandy-colored hair curled on his forehead, accenting eyes that startled me. One was brown, the other blue.

"Peter, this is Deborah something. One of Brenda's friends. Deborah, Peter MacDonald. He's a poet. Does odd jobs instead of paying rent."

Peter reached out a hand to shake mine. "Hello, Deborah something. I saw you and your friends yesterday. Surprised me. Brenda doesn't often have company."

"Never mind that," said Esther. "These girls need some rakes to clean up Brenda's yard."

"Where's Leroy?" Peter's voice was cadenced, as if he spoke with the rhythms of his poems.

"Leroy's gone," I said.

"Gone? I can't get that tree limb cleared by myself." Peter pointed toward a limb that had fallen in front of Esther's other rental unit. "Good thing it missed the cottage."

Esther folded her arms across her waist. The position highlighted the stain on her sweatshirt that sat on a chest flattened with age. "Cottage is empty. You know that. Tenants Gerald found canceled. Not the first time that's happened. I'll expect him to reimburse me when he gets back." Her annoyance showed in her clipped sentences.

"Gerald's not coming back." I decided it was time for Esther to learn the truth.

Peter stepped away from the door and stood next to Esther. He towered over her like a young warrior ready to defend an aged woman. "First Leroy. Now Gerald. Where'd they go?"

"The sheriff," said Esther. Her voice was strong. She didn't need defending. "It was about Gerald. Is he hurt or dead?"

"Dead," I said.

Esther unfolded her arms. With her back hunched under her sweatshirt and her green eyes staring at me from behind her huge glasses, she looked like a frightening character in a fairy tale. "Dead how?"

"I'm afraid he was murdered."

Peter put his arm around Esther. "Poor Brenda."

Esther pulled away. "Poor? Lucky's a better word. He was a bastard."

* *

Brenda surprised me when she said she liked gardening. The only reason she left it to others was because of Gerald. He didn't like neighbors seeing his wife working. The moment she stepped outside into the sun she seemed freer, more like the Brenda of our childhood.

Anyone who could see us from the window of a distant house or who drove by would wonder where Gerald had found a crew of women for yard work. Brenda wore jeans and a T-shirt that were covered in paint. She'd tucked her hair under a wide-brimmed straw hat and was kneeling in the flower garden clipping dead and damaged blossoms. I worked next to her while Rachel and Krista raked up debris and packed it into the trash barrel.

Brenda glanced at them. She tossed aside a handful of dead blossoms. "Rachel and Krista should have been Mutt and Jeff, not Krista and me. Rachel liked that Cleopatra nickname too much. She always was the glamorous one." Brenda's resentment of Rachel was palpable. If Rachel felt it, she might accuse Brenda of murder the way she had suggested it to me last night. I vowed not to let them be alone together.

"I used to think of you both as sophisticated," I said, trying to deflect Brenda's jealousy. "Something I wanted to be. I tried growing my hair long but I could never blow-dry it so it looked good. My ponytail was about as glamorous as Esther's bun."

"Don't make fun of Esther. She's my only friend." She shook some leaves off a zinnia blossom that hadn't been damaged.

"We're here. We'll help you get through this."

"You and Krista will. I shouldn't have invited Rachel." She cut off the zinnia blossom she'd just saved and crumpled it. Her fingers were stained, her nail polish as damaged as the flowers.

"Why did you invite us?"

"A whim, I guess. A chance to show that I've come a long way since I was the poorest of us."

"Were you afraid of Gerald?" I wondered if her real motive was to seek our help.

She speared her clippers into the dirt. "No. I didn't even realize how much he controlled me until we all got together. Now it doesn't matter. Gerald's dead." She stood up and wiped off her jeans. "Looks like Scotty's here. Will you come inside with me? I'm afraid of what they found out."

"Should Rachel and Krista come?"

"Too many people. Scotty will tell me when to go to Berkinshaw's. I'll want you with me. You're the one who's had a husband die."

We met Sheriff Holland and another police officer at the back of the house.

Brenda spoke directly. "Did you find out who killed my husband?"

"Not yet." Holland took off the hat he'd been wearing last night. It still looked damp, but it wasn't dripping water. "This is Bashiir Abu." Abu was tall with a thin body and black skin. His name identified him as one of the Somalis who'd settled in Maine and who were being recruited by various police departments.

Brenda looked at Abu. "Why are you here?"

Holland answered for him. "He's a detective from the state police homicide unit. They need to be involved in the investigation."

"Come inside. I'll get us coffee." Brenda spoke as if they were friends come for a visit until I heard the catch in her voice when she said, "Can Deborah stay with me?"

"Of course," said Holland. "You're not being investigated."

Brenda led us inside to the table, forgetting her offer of coffee.

The salt and pepper shakers from our oyster dinner were unmoved, a reminder of Gerald's odd habit of collecting them. She twirled the death's head pepper shaker while she listened to Sheriff Holland. Abu sat beside him, taking notes.

"We checked all the golf resorts in Hilton Head. Gerald or someone canceled his reservation a week ago. Whoever took the cancellation didn't remember if the voice was male or female." Holland looked at Brenda. "Did he drive to his boat? His car's not there or here."

"He left it at Corey's for its annual tune-up. Nelson Sproul drove him to the airport."

"We also checked the airlines. That reservation was canceled, so he wouldn't have gone there."

"That's where he told me he was going. I never woke up when he left. Nelson drove him somewhere."

"We stopped at the oyster farm this morning. Nelson said he didn't drive him anywhere."

Brenda began sprinkling little bits of pepper on the uncovered table. "Are you telling me Gerald lied?"

"Maybe you just misunderstood him." Sheriff Holland sounded conciliatory. "Do you know if he had any enemies?"

"Everybody loved Gerald," said Brenda.

I wanted to say except Esther Sproul.

"What about money?" Holland continued his questioning. "Any unpaid debts?"

Brenda slammed the pepper shaker on the table. It fell on its side, spilling a line of black along a groove on the table. "How would I know. He lied to me about a golf weekend. What am I supposed to think?"

I picked up the pepper shaker and moved it away from Brenda, forcing myself to stay quiet. I wanted to tell Holland and Abu about Brenda's suspicion that Gerald was involved in something illegal, wanted to tell them about the sudden appearance of the O'Donnells as live-in help, wanted to tell him that Nelson Sproul might be somehow connected.

Holland approached the predictable topic. "Might he be having an affair?"

Brenda took off the hat she was still wearing and tossed her hair. "He might have lied about golf, but I'd know if he were having an affair."

From the way Brenda had been describing Gerald, I doubted her.

"What about the O'Donnells?" said Holland. "You told me last night that they left and took Gerald's tools. Could he have gone with them?"

"No. Gerald left before dawn on Thursday. They were here on Friday when my friends arrived. Deborah saw them leave in the middle of the night."

Holland addressed me, "When did you see them leave?"

"I was in the bathroom around one o'clock. I remember because I looked at my cell phone when I got some Advil. When I came back into the bedroom, I saw the truck parked in front of the Sproul's."

Abu let Holland do all the questioning while he took notes, I assumed because the sheriff was the one who knew the people involved. "Did anyone get into it?"

"Not that I saw," I said.

"Could you tell who was driving?" Holland continued. "See how many people were in the cab?"

"I'm sorry. It was dark and I wasn't wearing glasses."

Holland addressed Brenda. "Do you know where Gerald found Leroy and Maureen? Didn't you use to hire local help in the summer?"

Brenda rubbed off a piece of flower that had caught in the

diamond she wore on her left hand. "He didn't tell me. They've been here for three years. They stay all winter."

Holland glanced at Abu. "We know that much. Did he ever call them by different names?"

"What are you suggesting?" said Brenda.

"Nothing. Just trying to follow through on where they might have gone. Can a forensics team look in the cottage? We can get a warrant, but it's the Fourth and it would take some time."

"They won't find anything. Leroy and Maureen took all their things along with Gerald's tools. Even took the toilet paper."

Holland pushed back his chair and motioned to Abu. "Forensics is here now."

"I'm not stupid, Scotty." Brenda rose to stand next to his imposing bulk. "You think Maureen and Leroy are connected to Gerald's murder."

"If they are, we'll find out. Could be a coincidence. Can we search?"

"If they're here already, you assumed I'd let you. Go ahead. Sorry I forgot the coffee."

They left me to finish with the yard clean-up. I moved the croquet set that Rachel and Krista had put at the edge of the porch. It was soaked, making me wish we had put it away when we returned from Monhegan Island. I wheeled it through an opening I saw under the porch. It hit something. I pulled it out again and bent to see what was blocking it. There was just enough light for me to see that a pile of rakes had been pushed in front of a lawnmower. Maureen and Leroy hadn't stolen all of the tools. If this was the usual storage place, close to the lawn and garden, Brenda shouldn't have been so quick to accuse them of theft.

I heard the sheriff's car pull onto the road and motioned to Brenda as she came around the side of the house. I showed her what was under the porch. "There are garden tools here. Were there more in the shed?"

"How should I know? I never go into the shed. All I know is they cleaned out the house. The forensics people are still looking but they won't find anything." She started toward the porch steps. "Push that croquet set in. It will fit. It always does."

CHAPTER 7

"WOULD YOU LIKE to view his body before you make a final decision?" Dressed in a black suit and white shirt, Daniel Berkinshaw looked the part of a mortician. He'd gone over details with us about funeral costs, obituaries, death certificates.

"Okay, but I won't be buying a fancy coffin," said Brenda.

Berkinshaw stood up. "Do you want to go in alone?"

"No. Deborah will come with me. How bad does he look?"

"Pretty bad. We cleaned him up as much as we could unless you want us to work on his face for a viewing."

"That won't be necessary."

At the end of a long hallway, Berkinshaw opened the door into the part of the funeral home that served as a mortuary. He pointed to a lone gurney where a body lay covered in a sheet, then closed the door so we could be alone.

Brenda stood over the body, her lips moving silently. I thought she was praying. After several minutes, she took a corner of the sheet in her hand then slowly lowered it. She choked back a gasp. "I thought I'd like seeing him this way."

The pressure of tears rose behind my eyes at memories of Nathan and Cathy lying on separate gurneys so many years ago. Cathy had only a single bruise on her temple. She could have been sleeping. I'd wanted to pick her up, cradle her in my arms.

As much as the mortician had tried, he couldn't disguise the damage done to Nathan's face.

Gerald looked even worse. I could see why the police had trouble identifying him. His face was covered in cuts that had been washed. His hair had been combed over a misshapen forehead and the place where his nose had been was a gaping hole. His jaw was angled so his upper and lower lips were off center.

Brenda touched his closed eyes. "He had beautiful eyes. Their blue reminded me of Joseph Wheeler's. I think that's why I married him." She pulled the sheet over his face and went to the door. Daniel Berkinshaw stood in the hallway, waiting for us.

"Burn him." Brenda used the same tone she had with Sheriff Holland. Whatever love she must once have felt for Gerald had hardened in the cold rather than warmed in a fire.

A note lay on the dining room table under a salt shaker that looked like Moby Dick. Brenda handed it to me. I recognized Rachel's handwriting, the near calligraphy of an artist. All it said was that she and Krista had gone for a walk.

"You can go look for them if you want," said Brenda. "I don't have the energy. I'm going for a nap." She left me standing alone.

I went onto the front porch where I could hear seagulls squawking in the distance. The two rakes I'd borrowed rested on a boulder at the side of the storm-decimated garden, their tines facing upward in a way my father always warned me against. I'd return the rakes that looked like weapons later.

I went upstairs to exchange my sandals for sneakers. The door to Brenda's studio was closed. A framed print of the Calderwood crest hung on it. The same band of blue with white stars, the same red X, the same helmet with the visor down that I'd seen when I first arrived. I wanted to lift the visor, see what secrets Gerald held that caused him to be murdered.

The socks I'd worn in the morning were draped over my suitcase, drying, so I rummaged in the suitcase for another pair. I wrapped a sun protecting shirt around my waist. The mid-afternoon sun wouldn't be strong, but the breeze might be cool.

I left the door to my room open and paused in front of the crest on Brenda's door, listening for any sign that she was inside, that she might finally have cried for the husband she barely grieved. It was silent. My sneakers were quiet on the stairs.

On the porch, I let the sun chase away the oppressive silence of the house and walked across the grass onto the road that led to the ocean. Summer houses, some white, some with weathered shingles, were tucked among boulders or behind trees, all distant from one another. This was not a neighborhood where people talked over picket fences. All the yards had been cleaned of debris from last night's storm. In only one did I see a group of children kicking a soccer ball.

A sign at the edge of a long driveway read *Calderwood Beach Club*. Beneath it a red, white, and blue banner announced *July 4th Celebration 4:00*. That explained the quiet. Club members were inside their houses resting or planning their wardrobes. At the bottom of the hill that led to the Club, I could see someone raising an American flag on a pole that stood in front of the clubhouse. The flag stopped at half-mast. Club members must have learned about Gerald's death, but it wasn't going to stop their Fourth of July celebration. Under a canopy of lights, I could just make out a platform filled with a drum set and amplifiers.

I continued further along the road that narrowed from asphalt to dirt. It dead-ended at a small parking area empty of cars. A sign that said *Beach* pointed me to the right. I walked down a rocky path, glad of my sneakers. The beach was sheltered in a tiny cove so only a ripple of waves broke on the rocky shore. There was no level sand to spread a blanket on. No one had built sand castles, but various stone mini-towers showed that cairns weren't forbidden the way they were on Monhegan Island.

Rachel sat against a small boulder, her knees bent to prop up a sketchbook. Krista was standing at the edge of the beach skipping stones in water that was so sheltered it was almost smooth even after the storm. I joined her and picked up a flat smooth one. "Do they skip well?"

She answered with the technique I remembered she'd had when we were kids. Six skips. I tried mine. It plopped into the water.

"It's all in the wrist." She demonstrated, this time getting five skips.

I found another stone and tried again. One feeble skip.

"Better." She bent to collect a handful of stones. "Was it awful at the funeral parlor?"

"Pretty bad. I could barely look at Gerald his face was so battered."

"What about Brenda? Did she finally break down?" Krista chose one of the stones she was holding in her left hand.

"She was pretty calm. She brought up Joseph Wheeler again. Said she married Gerald because his eyes were as blue as Joseph's."

Krista flicked the stone into the water for only four skips. "I'm surprised she invited Rachel. I can still feel the rivalry that started over Joseph when we were juniors."

"I think she was remembering further back when she invited us. Maybe even to elementary school." I accepted a stone from Krista and tried another skip. The stone hit the water and sunk along with the hopes I'd had for a joyful reunion with old friends.

"Did she make funeral arrangements?" said Krista. "I wonder if we'll still be here."

"Not yet. She's having Gerald cremated." Brenda's "burn him" reverberated like the five skips Krista achieved with her next stone.

She rinsed her hands in the water and wiped them on her shorts. "I suppose she'll still have some kind of service. People will expect it and she'll be able to play the grieving widow."

"That's a bit harsh. Not like you."

"I know, but I can't figure her out. One minute she praises Gerald—"

I interrupted. "Not him. The lifestyle he gave her."

"And one she can keep. She's not exactly overwhelmed with grief."

Someone coming down the path to the beach interrupted our conversation. At first I thought it was Leroy. He had the same shock of red hair, but he was as skinny as an anorexic. He looked unhealthy. As he came closer, I recognized him as the man I'd glimpsed on Monhegan Island.

He stopped beside us and set his bicycle on the sand. It was loaded with enough gear that he might have been on a camping trip. "Good skippin'?" he said, dropping his "g" in a way I always found annoying.

I stepped away from him. He smelled of marijuana.

"Want some?" he asked, pulling a joint out of the pocket of a torn flannel shirt.

"We're just leaving." Krista had moved even further away than I had.

"Her, too?" He gestured toward Rachel.

"She'll come with us," I said. We left the man at the edge of the water and joined Rachel. Her sketch wasn't of the calm cove in front of her. Instead she'd imagined a turbulent sea and a capsized sailboat. At the base of a rocky cliff, a few black lines suggested a body washed ashore.

She tore off the page and tucked it into the back of her sketchbook. "Do you think Brenda murdered him?" Rachel repeated what she'd said last night. The idea had been hovering at the edge of my consciousness all day.

"Of course not. She was with us."

Rachel glanced at the man who was now sitting cross-legged on the rocky beach. "Is that Leroy? He's involved."

"It's not Leroy," I said, wondering who the young man might be. We didn't know Gerald's time of death. I knew Leroy could have killed him before we arrived or after he and Maureen disappeared. Could he also have involved the man with his shade of red hair?

Krista took Rachel's sketchbook and reached for her arm to help her to her feet. "Brenda's our friend. She's not a killer."

Rachel took back her sketchbook. "I suppose you're right. Brenda's a lot of things. Jealous. Dependent. Self-centered. But she's never been violent."

She left out "cruel."

From a distance, I could see Esther sitting on her side porch. When I crossed the street, a rake in each hand, I expected to find an old woman hunched and asleep over an unraveling piece of knitting. Instead, she sprang out of her chair and fixed me with her green eyes. "Leave the rakes here and come inside. Help me with Nelson's computer."

She set the book she'd been reading onto her chair. *A Murder is Announced.* I recognized the title as an Agatha Christie novel and wanted to call Esther Miss Marple. She looked like whoever played the character on the old PBS series.

I followed her up a staircase to a room on the third floor. Despite her curved spine, her step was firm and she had no need to hold onto the railing. We went into a room set up with two desks, a computer on one, a bookkeeper's ledger on the other. They faced windows where Esther could see anything happening at Brenda's house.

"Sit." She directed me to the chair in front of the computer and rolled the other chair beside me. She pressed the on button. The sign *Sproul's Oyster Farm* filled the screen. A rectangle asked me for a password.

"Why are we doing this?" I said. "Do you think Nelson's involved in something?"

"Of course not. He's my son. I'm worried about the business." She removed her glasses and wiped them on a tissue she took out of the pocket of the yellow sweatshirt she wore in the morning. "Try some passcode things."

"Give me some hints."

Her Maine accent emerged as she fired ideas at me, all related to oyster farming. "Brookstock." "Hatchery." "Microalgae." "Crassostrea Virginica."

"Spell that one."

"C-r-a-s-s-o-s-t-r-e-a. Then Virgin plus i-c-a. It's the name for the Eastern oyster."

I gave up and explained why this wouldn't work. "Besides an infinite number of words and deciding how to capitalize, we'd have to figure out numbers or symbols like a parenthesis or colon or quotation mark. What did you think you'd find?"

"Something in that email stuff people do. Isn't that what all the fuss was about with Hillary Clinton?"

"And nothing came if it." If I knew Esther's politics, I would have added "Except a botched election and a country in turmoil."

She said it for me. "Should have elected her. Saved us all that climate change denial that's going to destroy the oyster business. I'm afraid I won't live to see a woman president."

"I think you will." Esther reminded me of the Energizer Bunny. Her batteries would never die.

She wheeled her chair back to the desk that I assumed was hers. "Look at the view I have of the Calderwood house. I see things."

"Is that why you think Nelson knew something about Gerald?"

"It happened a week ago. Gerald had croquet set up and was practicing. He cheats, you know. Like that guy in *Little Women*."

"I remember that scene. A friend of Laurie's. It shocked me when I was a kid. Odd that we both still remember it."

"I read that book a dozen times. Never could figure out why Jo married that old man professor instead of Laurie. Same as I can't figure out why Brenda married a cheat like Gerald." She pushed on the arms of her chair to stand up.

I joined her and looked out the window. "What did you see besides Gerald practicing croquet?"

"Nelson went over there last Sunday. He was yelling and waving some kind of envelope at Gerald. Nelson can be grumpy but he doesn't yell. That's what Gerald does. If I turn on my hearing aids, I can hear him yelling at Brenda. He's a mean one, that Gerald."

"Was," I said. "Why do you think Nelson was angry?"

"When I asked, he just said nothing for me to worry about. But it was something important. Gerald grabbed the envelope from Nelson, ripped it up, and threw the pieces at him. When Nelson left, I watched Gerald collect the pieces. He walked to the side of the house—the side I can see—and threw them into the trash can. Leroy was getting ready to take the cans to the dump. We can't fish through it."

Even if we could, I wouldn't have fished through trash. "You should tell the police what you saw. They'll talk to Nelson."

"No need for police." Hunched in front of the window, she'd

transformed from the Energizer Bunny to a woman old and weighed down.

I wondered why she would avoid the police. Was she afraid that her son was involved? I touched her waist and turned her away from the window. "Don't worry. Whatever was going on with Gerald will come out."

She flashed her eyes at me. She'd come alive again and looked defiant. "Maybe not. Let's get those rakes back to Peter. He's a good person."

"Brenda thinks so. She told me to ask him to drive me to The Lobster Landing. We'll cook the lobsters Maureen was supposed to fix for us."

"Those two. Maureen and Leroy. Gone missing. Gerald was always going in and out of that cottage. Whatever he was involved in, they were, too."

Peter's car was something a starving poet would own, one of the Volkswagen Beetles the company rolled out in the nineties to reinvent itself until its manipulation of diesel exhaust tests caused it to lose its reputation. The car was black, like an actual beetle. A noise came from the passenger side, sounding like the high screech of a bug.

"Sorry about the screech. I need to take Dylan some place to be serviced." He used a name he'd given to his car.

"You named it after Bob Dylan?"

"Dylan Thomas. I like all those Celtic rhythms."

"Isn't Calderwood a Celtic name?" I said. "I see the crest all over Brenda's house."

"Scottish. Gerald did like to brandish around his connection to the Scotch settlers in this area." Peter swerved to avoid hitting a tabby cat.

"What was Gerald like? Do you have any idea why someone would kill him?"

Peter lost the poetic lilt in his voice when he said, "Gerald was a bastard."

"You've been here long enough to know that?"

"I knew him in Boston."

"I'm surprised. It doesn't seem like Gerald would travel with poets."

"I used to park his car when he went to The Algonquin Club. He didn't talk to me much, but his wife did. I knew they summered in Maine. One day I asked her if she could help me find a place I could escape to and concentrate on my writing. I've been here since May."

"So it's here that you decided that he's a bastard?"

"Was. Brenda's better off without him."

"Still, it's hard to lose a husband. Something worked in their marriage."

"It's called money." Peter slowed as we came to what passed for a main street in Bristol. "His murder's connected to the oyster farm."

"How do you know that?"

He pulled into a parking lot in front of The Lobster Landing, turning off the car screech that had been vibrating in my head. "I notice things. Go get your lobsters. Did you ask for them to be cooked?"

"No. We all know how to cook lobsters. We thought it might ease the tension in the house, maybe even be fun."

He faced me with his unsettling brown and blue eyes. "Put them alive into boiling water and watch them die."

CHAPTER 8

I PUT THE lobsters in the refrigerator and looked outside on the porch. No one was there, so I went upstairs to check. Krista's room was empty. Rachel's was open. She was standing in front of her window, as motionless as a statue. I stepped quietly into the room. "Are you okay?"

She turned to me. "I'm fine."

Her straight hair fell to her shoulders and the blunt cut of her bangs skimmed her eyebrows. If she'd put on a headband like the ones she wore in high school, I would have called her Cleopatra the way we did thirty years ago. She looked beautiful, but pensive. She'd seen too much of death. We both had.

I sat on the edge of the bed and patted the space next to me. "Come sit. I'll tell you about Esther."

She got onto the bed and leaned against the headboard. I swung my legs onto the bed and slid next to her. Through the window, I could see Esther's house bathed in light from the late day sun. "The lobsters are in the refrigerator. At least tonight we'll eat before dark so we'll finish to watch the fireworks."

"Hard to care about fireworks. What about Esther?"

I bent my knees and wrapped my arms around them. "She wanted me to hack into Nelson's computer. The only passcodes she fed me involved oysters."

Rachel bent her legs in a twin position with my own except for their extra six inches. "That would make sense. He owns an oyster farm. Did you find anything?"

"I'm not a computer hacker. She told me she saw Nelson give Gerald an envelope last Sunday. Gerald tore it up."

"Does she think her son killed Gerald?"

"More likely she thinks Nelson knows something about Gerald and the O'Donnells."

"We're staying next door to a murderer."

"You mean Nelson?"

"Or Esther."

"Don't be ridiculous. She's an old woman. But there's something else."

She leaned her head and shoulders forward. Her hair draped around her knees so she looked like a cornered animal. She straightened and said, "What else?"

"Esther said the argument happened when Gerald was practicing croquet. The set's stored under the porch steps. Brenda must know the tools are also stored there. It's a tight fit."

"So Brenda lied about the O'Donnells stealing the tools?"

"Maybe there were extra tools." I wanted to think that.

She pushed away from the headboard and swung her legs over the side of the bed. "We should leave. We might be staying with a murderer."

"Brenda didn't invite us here so she could kill her husband. Gerald really had plane and hotel reservations when she invited us. We need to stay."

"Why?"

"She was our friend. Don't forget the past."

"I wish I could."

"She has no reason to kill us and it's only one more day. What time's your flight out on Tuesday?" I got off the bed and picked up

Rachel's flight itinerary that was on the bedside table. Her arrival time in Portland stood out at the top of the page. Wednesday June 30. Arrives 8:15 PM. A wave of nausea found its way from my stomach to my throat.

Rachel got off the bed and walked around to where I was holding her itinerary. She took it away from me and put it on the table. "I was going to tell you. I needed to prepare."

"Prepare for what?"

"For seeing Brenda again. We weren't exactly friends our senior year."

"I could have come earlier and stayed with you."

"Like I said, I needed to prepare. Portland's a lovely city." She went to the window and stood looking out the way I'd seen her when I came into the room.

Krista appeared at the doorway and broke the silence that had descended between us. "What have you two been up to? I've been out walking."

Rachel moved away from the window. "Just talking. What time is it?"

"After six," said Krista. "Let's go cook those lobsters."

And watch them die, I thought, remembering Peter's words.

The water was boiling for the lobsters. It was too early in the season for corn, so potatoes were baking. Rachel and I were making a salad while Krista was setting the table. Brenda was across the street accepting a blueberry pie Esther had offered.

Everything was ready except the lobsters when Brenda came into the kitchen carrying the pie. It was gorgeous, spots of blueberry juice seeping onto a crust perfectly crimped on the edges.

"Esther makes beautiful pies." I took it from Brenda and set it on the counter in front of the coffee pot, glad we could drink coffee instead of black tea with it.

"She loves to bake." Brenda took dessert plates out of her cupboard and stacked them next to the pie. "Five. One for Esther. She'll come over to watch the fireworks."

"She's an interesting woman," said Krista, who'd finished with the table and was washing off the cutting boards we'd been using.

"Interesting and interested," said Brenda. "She was full of questions about Gerald. I don't want to talk about him." She pulled the lid off the lobster pot. "Water's boiling."

Brenda took the bag from the refrigerator. She lifted out a lobster and plunged it into the boiling water. "This one's Leroy." The second one she named "Maureen," the third "Nelson." When she held the last one over the pot, she looked at Rachel. I was afraid she was going to say her name. She dipped the head of the lobster into the pot, pulled it back, and looked at its eyes. "Gerald." She dropped it into the water. "Boil away," she said as she put the lid onto the pot.

The lobster, as red as Leroy's hair, stared at us. I reached for a lobster cracker and saw that there were none on the table. "Do you have lobster crackers? I asked Brenda, who was sitting across from me. She looked accusingly at Krista, who was next to her. "Guess Krista forgot them."

I pushed back my chair. "I'll get them. Where are they?"

"Top drawer next to the sink."

I went into the kitchen and opened the drawer. Two wooden cases looked like they held lobster tools. I picked up one, opened it, and dropped it on the floor. It held oyster shucking knives. One was missing.

I picked it up and put it back into the drawer, my hand shaking as much as Brenda's. I found the lobster tools and carried them in their case to the dining room. I walked around the table, placing a cracker and a tiny fork at each place. When I got to Brenda, I said, "I opened the wrong box first. Do you know you have an oyster shucking knife missing?"

Rachel's hand found a strand of hair. She understood what I was asking.

"It broke and I threw it away. Gerald promised to buy me a new set. Sit down. These lobsters are waiting to be eaten."

I went back into the kitchen and put the box on the counter, taking deep breaths to lower my pulse that had gone into overdrive. Brenda sounded convincing. But maybe Rachel was right. I needed to ask the police what kind of weapon stabbed Gerald.

When I took my place at the table, everyone had started to crack their lobsters. I pulled a claw off mine, broke it at the joint, removed the small pincher and cracked the larger one. The shell was soft. We didn't even need lobster crackers. I could almost break it apart with my fingers. I dipped the meat into the butter and took my first bite.

Rachel mirrored me. "I haven't had a boiled lobster in thirty years," said Rachel. "Crawfish in New Orleans. They're good, but nothing like this."

I didn't mention the lobster rolls on Monhegan or the lobster stew Rachel and I ate at Clive's Chowder House when we'd discovered the details about Joseph Wheeler's death. I cracked out another piece of lobster meat, hoping I wouldn't start to think of murder every time I ate a lobster.

Krista started on her second claw. "If I lived in Maine, I'd eat lobster a couple of times a week."

Brenda let some lobster meat soak in her ramekin of butter while she drank the last of the wine in her glass. "In Colonial times, the rich were told not to feed servants lobster more than three times a week. Lobsters used to pile up on the shoreline. It was fed to prisoners and the poor."

"How do you know that?" Krista said as she broke off the tail of her lobster.

Brenda refilled her glass. "Esther. She's always talking about what we've done to the environment."

"She's worried about the oyster farm," I said.

Krista paused in cutting the meat from her lobster tail. "Maybe we shouldn't eat lobster. She's right to worry. I don't eat cod now because of overfishing."

"Peter talked about the oyster farm when we were buying the lobsters. He thinks Gerald's death has some connection." I phrased what I said carefully.

Brenda was blunt. "You mean his murder. Peter's right. It connects to that oyster farm. Not to fancy oyster shucking knives."

She knew what I'd been thinking when I asked about the missing knife.

Krista stared at Brenda from behind the glasses with the mottled yellow frame that she wore inside. "Why do you say that?"

Brenda broke off her lobster tail, splattering a puddle of juice onto her plate. "When we were in Boston, he'd get calls from Nelson. He doesn't even like him."

"Esther saw them fighting a week ago," I said. "She thinks Nelson knows something."

Brenda tossed a shell into the bowl we'd centered in front of us on the table. "Esther's too damned nosy. If Gerald was involved in something, Nelson still is."

A call to Brenda's landline interrupted us. She went into the kitchen to answer the phone that hung on a wall. We all could hear her talking on the old technology. "What money?" "Who is this?" "Why call me?" "I don't know what you're talking about." She slammed the receiver down and came back into the dining room.

She refilled her wine glass before she spoke. Her tremor was stronger than it had been all evening. "Whoever it was said he'd tried Gerald's cell phones."

"Phones? Plural?" I said.

Brenda broke off one of the small claws and sucked at it. "That's what he said. They're probably at the bottom of the ocean."

"What did he want?" said Krista.

Brenda sucked at another claw. "Money. He said Gerald owes him five grand."

I remembered Esther's comment about the Irish mafia. "Did he actually say grand?"

"Forget it. Let's just finish our lobsters before Esther gets here. Anybody want eggs and tamale? Why do I always get a lobster filled with wax?" She scraped the tamale and eggs onto the edge of her plate. The waxy red eggs next to the green tamale looked like an angry splatter on one of her paintings.

CHAPTER 9

COMING THROUGH THE doorway, Esther could have been dressed for a poster that promoted patriotism. She wore a navy blue lounge suit with American flags running in a straight line along each side of the zipper. She'd attached a red ribbon to her bun. It hung lopsided to her neck.

"Let me fix your ribbon." Brenda took her hand and helped her into the dining room. She showed a gentleness that made me realize that she liked Esther even though she complained about her being nosy.

"Can't lift my arms the way I used to." Esther demonstrated by raising her arms. They stopped below her shoulders.

"Did Nelson put this ribbon in your hair?" Brenda removed bobby pins and the ribbon from Esther's bun. She tied the ribbon into a neat bow and reattached it.

"Nelson's at the Club. Peter helped me." Esther shook her head so the ends of the ribbon glided along the base of her hairline. She wore the kind of coy expression I sometimes saw on old women.

"I hope Peter's a better poet than he is a hairdresser," I said.

"I haven't seen any of his poy-try." Esther pronounced poetry the way I remembered my grandmother doing.

Esther took a seat at the head of the table in front of the

blueberry pie. "Good we're eating inside. Mosquitoes are out. There won't be as many after dark when the fireworks begin."

"Coffee or tea?" I said.

"Tea," said Esther. "That black kind Brenda keeps for me."

"I'll help you," said Rachel. "Krista, one of those herbal teas?"

"Thanks. The decaf peppermint I saw in the cabinet." Krista sat in one of the chairs closest to Esther.

"No coffee or tea for me," said Brenda. "Wine goes well with blueberry pie."

Rachel and I went into the kitchen. It smelled of lobster shells. I readjusted the lid on the trash can. "I'll empty this after we finish dessert. Otherwise the smell will be awful in the morning."

"Let me see those oyster knives." She opened the kitchen drawer and the case then picked up the remaining knife. "Would the blade be long enough to kill a man?"

"I don't know."

"We need to tell the police."

"I will. Bring in the dessert and I'll call the sheriff."

Rachel found five mugs in the cabinet. They all showed the Calderwood crest. "I don't get it," she said.

"Get what?"

"This whole weekend. Brenda complains about Esther being nosy. Now she's acting like she's Esther's mother. Why is Esther asking a poet handyman to help her with that ridiculous ribbon instead of going to the Fourth of July celebration at the beach club?"

"We can ask her."

Rachel poured water into the mugs for Krista and Esther. "I hope I don't mix them up," she said as she brought them into the dining room.

I'd left my phone in my room, so I went to the phone on the wall, called information, and got connected. A female voice answered. "Lincoln Country Sheriff's Department. Can I help you?"

"Could I speak with Sheriff Holland?"

"One moment."

When she connected me to Holland, I told him about the missing oyster knife. "You said Gerald Calderwood had been stabbed. Would an oyster knife have been long enough?"

"I can't give you any details. But thank you for the information. If anything else comes up, please let us know." His voice was non-committal.

I felt like I was betraying a friend when I picked up the coffee pot in one hand and the two mugs for Rachel and me in the other. When I came into the dining room, Brenda said, "Did you find the ice cream?"

It was going to be a long night. I wanted to tell her that I wasn't her servant. Instead I put the coffee pot and mugs onto the table and went back into the kitchen for ice cream. The lobster smell overwhelmed the lingering smell of coffee.

The phone rang, startling me so much I dropped the ice cream scoop I'd found in a drawer below the one with the seafood tools. After five rings and no sign that Brenda was going to answer the phone, I lifted the receiver half expecting to hear Sheriff Holland's voice. "Calderwood residence."

"Who's this? I'm lookin' for Gerald."

The man who spoke dropped his gs the way the man we'd seen on the beach had done.

"I'm a friend of Brenda's. Did I see you on the beach earlier?"

"No reason for me to be hangin' on that beach. You goin' to get Gerald for me?"

I was sure the voice belonged to the same man. Whoever he was, he hadn't heard about Gerald's death. I wasn't going to tell him. "Gerald's not here."

"Figures," he said, and hung up.

I picked the ice cream scoop off the floor, rinsed it, and took a half gallon of vanilla from the freezer. When I got into the dining room, Esther was cutting the pie. "It's better if I use wild Maine blueberries," she said, "but it's a little early for them. Peter took me to pick cultivated ones yesterday. He didn't help me pick, just sat on the grass writing a poem." She left one piece in the plate.

"Is that last piece for Nelson?" I said.

"For Peter. Nelson will have more sweets than he needs at the Club. You can be the scooper." Esther passed the cut pieces down the table.

I began scooping. "Don't you go to the Club on the Fourth?"

"Usually. I thought Brenda would want my company today."

Brenda scowled at Esther and swallowed some wine. "Was that Nelson on the phone checking up on her?"

"Nelson wouldn't check up on me. He's not like Gerald."

Krista tried to steer the conversation away from the tension that was building. "You make fabulous pie, Esther. Blueberry's as good as the strawberry rhubarb."

The berry Esther spilled on her sweatshirt blended into the navy blue. "You should pick berries tomorrow," she said. "I can make you blueberry scones."

I tried a first bite. Krista was right. It was delicious. Not too sweet, just a hint of lemon giving it tartness. I answered Brenda's question that still hung in the air. "I think the call was from a man we saw on the beach. He had the same red hair as Leroy, but he was really skinny. Have you ever seen him? He might be a relative."

Esther pounced. "I've seen him around all week. He must go to the beach because he rides a bike from that direction, stops at our houses, and rides away from the Cove. I almost called Scotty Holland about him, but the man wasn't doing anything. I asked

Leroy. He just said 'Lots of people have red hair.' Maybe this bike rider killed Gerald."

I stopped her Miss Marple speculations. "He didn't know Gerald was dead. He asked for him."

"Forget him. Whoever he is, he's not from around here." Brenda stabbed her fork into her pie. "Finish your pie so we don't miss the fireworks."

I volunteered to empty the trash while everyone else went onto the porch to wait for the fireworks to begin. Already the lobster shells smelled of rotting fish and I wondered how something that tasted so good could disintegrate so quickly. I pulled the plastic bag out of the can and tied it tightly.

Outside the night had fallen. Fireflies accompanied the sound of crickets in the grass. I found the trash can behind the shed that had held Gerald's tools. The light from Brenda's back door barely illuminated it. A rustle beneath the roses that edged Brenda's parking spaces told me that some nocturnal animal had smelled a feast. I made sure the lid was firmly closed and hoped that whatever animal was waiting couldn't knock it off.

When I came away from the shed, a car pulled out of the driveway in back of Esther's house. The shape told me it was Peter's Volkswagen. The light from Brenda's house was enough that I could see someone was in the car with him. It sped away in the direction of town. Wherever Peter was going, it wasn't to the fireworks at the Calderwood Club.

The night had spooked me so much that when I opened the door, I jumped at the sound of the grandfather clock calling out nine. My heart rate quickened. By the time I stepped onto the porch it had slowed. Heartbeat of an athlete my doctor once told me. I was thankful for it now as I told myself there was no reason to think we were in danger.

The notes of a band playing "The Stars and Stripes Forever"

drifted through the air from Calderwood Cove. The music ended with the first burst of fireworks. A dance of arcs and flowers and waterfalls punctuated the stars. Red, yellow, orange, green, blue, the colors of an artist's palette exploded in myriad shapes.

Between each burst, Brenda directed a litany of memories to Esther. "When we were little, we ran around with sparklers in Deborah's yard. When the Shelby fire department set off fireworks at the lake, we'd spread blankets on the beach to watch. When we were teenagers, we'd party on the beach first." She raised her wine glass and drank as if our parties included drinking despite the town police hovering among us.

"Don't forget the mosquitoes." Krista swatted one.

The finale drowned out Brenda's last comment. It was something about Joseph Wheeler. The sky was a jeweled treasure chest that flickered and was gone. A skim of smoke lingered. As my ears adjusted to the quiet, I could hear the crickets again, shrilling in the grass.

We rose in unison. Inside, the house felt hot. Brenda walked to the table and poured the last of the wine into her glass. "Goodnight," she said and went into the bedroom she'd shared with Gerald.

"I'll walk you home," I said to Esther.

"No need," she said as she rescued the last of the pie she'd saved for Peter.

I took the pie from her. "Do you have a flashlight?"

"Forgot it." She held onto the table as she tried to straighten. The night had fatigued her. She was feisty and smart, but she still was a ninety-year-old woman.

"I saw one in the kitchen," said Krista. She left to get it and returned with one that looked as old as Esther.

Esther took it and switched it on. "This will do. Goodnight, ladies. I liked celebrating with you. When I spend Fourth of July at the Club, I have to turn my hearing aids off. Those explosions echo in my ears all night. This was nicer. I enjoyed hearing about how you all grew up together."

Rachel and Krista said goodnight and climbed the stairs to the bedrooms they were using. I followed Esther outside, careful to hold the pie plate so none of the juice spilled out. She lit the way to her unlocked door. I went inside with her and set the pie on the counter. Esther took the ribbon out of her hair and placed it next to the pie. Both looked forlorn.

"Do you need anything before I leave?"

"Course not. I've been living here for ninety years. I know my way around." She handed me the flashlight and pointed to the door.

I got half-way across the street when the batteries died. The sliver of moon and a sky full of stars lit my way. Behind the shed I heard an animal tip over the trash can. I shouted. Two raccoons came toward me, fixing me with their beady eyes. I shouted again and they disappeared into the night.

I woke to three gongs from the grandfather clock. A cool breeze blew through the open window, setting the curtains into a shadowy dance. I pulled the covers over my head and closed my eyes. Flashes of fireworks played on my eyelids. I was drifting back into sleep when I heard voices.

"Didn't find anythin' in the cottage." I recognized one voice. Whoever replied spoke so softly I couldn't identify if the voice was male or female.

Before I could throw off my covers, a car door slammed and one or both of the people drove away. The night went quiet except for the raucous squawks of seagulls protecting their nests.

CHAPTER 10

THE INCESSANT SQUAWKING of seagulls woke me. I put on my robe and went downstairs to fix myself a cup of coffee and enjoy the quiet on Brenda's porch. Mist rose from the grass, drifting into a cloudless sky. The air smelled of salt and sea grass. A hummingbird flitted around the flower garden where a few blossoms had come to life after the decimation of the storm.

The coffee jolted me into trying to make sense of the weekend. Brenda had built a life with a man who sounded at best controlling, at worst a criminal involved in something that got him killed. Esther and Peter both implied that the something involved Nelson Sproul's oyster farm. But how? And what did the O'Donnells have to do with it? Who were they? Where had they gone and why?

What about the red-haired man on the beach? He must have called Brenda and asked for money before he called a second time. He didn't know that Gerald Calderwood was dead. Who was he talking to in the middle of the night about going into the cottage? Even though I knew that G-men were FBI, I began thinking of him as the G-man because of his dropped *g*s and his demand for five grand.

I gave up thinking about the present and let myself drift into the past. Rachel, Krista, Brenda, and I had been the best of friends ever since that first day we met at Mrs. Wilkins' kindergarten. This was the school where we became the four inseparable girls we remained until Joseph Wheeler's death pulled us apart our senior year.

Mrs. Wilkins ran the school out of her house. Her backyard served as our playground. We made houses out of twigs and acorns that fell under a huge oak tree. Fairy houses like the ones we made two days ago on Monhegan Island. We'd pick clover at the side of our play area and use it to construct roofs. The memory made me think of Maureen and her shamrock tattoos. A thin, muscular woman with ash blond hair and an armload of tattoos driving in a truck with a burly red-haired man. They should be easy to find.

A crash from the back of the house near the shed made me spill the coffee that was jolting my brain into high speed. I climbed down the porch steps and grabbed a croquet mallet underneath it as if I were about to confront Leroy and Maureen instead of an early morning raccoon. When I reached the parking area, I saw a truck emblazoned with a sign that read Sproul's Oyster Farm.

Nelson appeared from behind the shed carrying the trash can. "You after a burglar or do you always play croquet in your bathrobe?"

I realized how silly I must look. My hair wasn't combed and my green bathrobe showed a coffee spill that rivaled Esther's dribbles of pie. "I thought it was a raccoon. I saw one last night trying to get into the trash can."

"Lobsters draw them. Put away the mallet. I'm taking the trash to the dump. I'll return the barrel tonight after work."

"Isn't there trash pickup?" I shouldn't have been surprised. There was no trash service in Shelby and Calderwood Cove was even smaller.

"Not unless you hire someone. It's Leroy's job. He usually goes on Sundays, but the dump was closed yesterday because of the Fourth. I refuse to call it the transfer station. The dump it was, the dump it still should be. I'm just helping out now that Leroy's gone."

"Do you know where he is? Why he left? The police said there's no forwarding address."

"Scotty Holland's useless. That Somali guy won't be worth much. Just filling a quota. Too many Somalis in Maine. I won't hire any."

I clutched the croquet mallet I held in one hand. The other held my coffee cup. I wanted to throw the few drops left into Nelson's face. I smiled when a seagull flew above us and dropped guano onto the windshield of his truck.

"Damn gulls." He lifted the trash can into the back of the truck. "Stop snooping around with my mother."

He got into his truck and sped away, leaving me to wonder if he knew that Esther and I had been trying to get into his computer.

I was pouring myself the third cup of coffee I didn't need when I heard two cars pull into Brenda's parking area. The clock on the coffee pot told me it was after nine. I carried my coffee to the open back door and looked through the screen. Bashiir Abu was stepping out of a state police car. He walked to a red Porsche and waited. I could see the driver talking on a cell phone. He got out of the car and slipped the phone into the pocket of his shirt. Scotty Holland. The two stood side by side, both six feet tall and towering over the low-slung Porsche.

I heard Holland say something about fingerprints as I opened the door. The stones on the pathway cut into my bare feet as I walked to them. "Have you found Gerald's killer?"

Holland shook the car keys he held in his left hand. "Just

returning Gerald's car. It was where Brenda said it was. Corey's Import Motors." He turned to Abu. "It's a beauty."

Abu touched the roof of the car. He shrugged as he withdrew his hand. I thought of Nelson's comment about Maine's Somalis. Without his state police uniform, Abu would be a target if he drove a red Porsche.

Holland continued to play with the keys. "Is Brenda available? We've got a few more questions."

"We're all on the front porch." I looked at my coffee mug. "Would you like coffee? There's a fresh pot."

"Love some," said Holland. Abu nodded agreement.

We went into the kitchen and I poured each of them a cup. "Milk and sugar?"

Both of them said no, so I handed them each a mug with the Calderwood crest. Holland looked at his. "Gerald sure liked to announce his ancestry. How's Brenda? Has she said anything that might help?"

"No, but Esther thinks Nelson knows something. He was arguing with Gerald last Sunday and waving a piece of paper at him. Gerald tore it up. Nelson collected the pieces and threw them away."

"We'll talk with him again. Who's Esther?" Abu put his mug on the counter to write something in the notebook he was carrying.

"Nelson Sproul's mother." I realized that Abu knew even less about Calderwood Cove than I did.

Holland used the back of his hand to rub a drip of coffee off his mouth. "Lives with Nelson in that big old summer house. She's ninety years old and knows everything about Calderwood Cove. She might know who picked Gerald up Thursday."

"She doesn't," I said.

Abu ignored me. "We'll talk with her." He picked up his mug and drank some coffee, then set it down again, still half full. "Is there anything else you can tell us before we talk with Brenda?"

"Brenda said that Nelson often called Gerald when they were in Boston. And Peter—I don't know his last name—thinks the oyster farm is connected somehow."

"Peter?" Abu spoke only to Holland.

Holland set his mug next to Abu's. His was empty. "Peter rents that old ship-building section attached to the Sproul house. Nelson had it renovated into an apartment that he rents out in the summer."

"It's Esther's house and she does the renting." I resented his assumption that a man had to be in charge.

Holland shrugged. "Doesn't matter."

Abu held his pen, ready to write. "Did Peter say why he thinks the oyster farm is involved?"

I tried to remember our conversation. "All he told me was that Brenda recommended the apartment. He's a poet and needed a place to write over the summer. He does odd jobs in lieu of rent."

"Gerald never let Brenda out. How in hell did she meet a poet?" Holland forgot he was a sheriff, not a friend.

Abu waved his hand to silence him. "We'll interview Peter. Find out why he thinks there's a connection. Anything else you can tell us?"

"Peter drove out with someone before the fireworks started. I don't think that means anything. But there was a stranger on the beach in the afternoon who offered us marijuana. Esther saw him several times last week riding a bicycle. When I first saw him on the beach, I thought he was Leroy. Same red hair but he's really skinny. He called Brenda last night, and around three this morning I heard him talking with someone outside."

"Did he give you his name?" Abu took more notes.

"No."

"How do you know he was the person on the phone?"

"I recognized his voice," I said. "He dropped his *gs.*"

"What's that mean?" said Holland.

"It's when someone says 'nothin' instead of 'nothing.'" Abu spoke with the precise enunciation of someone who'd worked hard to learn English.

"Weird thing to notice. Mind if I refill this?" Holland helped himself to more coffee. "Want a refill, Bashiir?"

"No, I've had enough." Abu continued to press me. "Could you tell who this stranger was talking with in the middle of the night?"

I wished I had gotten out of bed and looked out the window. "I couldn't even identify if the voice was male or female."

Abu put his pen in his shirt pocket. "How do we get to the front porch?"

"Follow me." Holland led us to the porch as if he'd visited often enough that he knew the house.

Rachel and Krista stood up, lined the railing, and looked down on Brenda. She started tapping the handle of her coffee mug with her ring. "Did you find him, Scotty?"

"Him?" Abu must have been pretending. It was obvious who Brenda meant.

Brenda got out of her chair and threw the remains of her coffee over the railing. "I was asking Scotty. Him. Gerald's killer."

Abu ignored the way Brenda cut him out of the investigation. "You assume a male killed your husband?"

This time Holland took the lead. "No, we haven't found him. Do you have any idea who might have picked Gerald up Thursday or where they might have taken his boat?"

Brenda spoke only to Holland. "If I knew that, Scotty, I would have told you yesterday. Why are you here? What did you find out?"

"We know that Gerald died sometime before noon on Thursday.

Whoever picked him up that morning must have driven him directly to his boat. We've found no one who was in the marina early and saw them."

Brenda continued to look only at Holland. "I bet it was Leroy." If she was lying, she was doing a good job of it.

Holland sipped coffee. "We've not located him or Maureen. They left no forwarding address."

"What about fingerprints in the cottage?" As soon as I said it, I knew I should stay quiet and just listen.

"We can't talk about an ongoing investigation." Unlike Holland, Abu was careful not to talk about the case.

Brenda ignored Abu. "You must have some ideas. A guy called me last night. Said Gerald owed him five grand."

"Any idea why Gerald would owe money?" Abu pressed Brenda.

Brenda leaned against the railing. "Tell him, Scotty. You knew Gerald. I know nothing about how he handled money. He never even let me have a credit card."

Abu looked shocked.

Holland ran his hand along the railing toward Brenda. "Everybody knows about that quirk of Gerald's. Brenda has plenty of credit at local stores."

Brenda moved away from Holland and spoke to Abu. "And always as much cash as I need. Gerald wasn't stingy."

"Gerald was a big spender. Generous with his money." Holland addressed Abu, then Brenda. "We'll figure out what happened. That mini safe I saw Leroy buying might be connected."

"That's enough." Again Abu reminded Holland that he was here as sheriff, not friend. "We'll come back when we hear something else. Call us if you remember anything." He handed Brenda a card. She brushed it away.

"I'll call you, Scotty." Brenda dismissed the two men by sitting down.

I walked Holland and Abu through the house and to the state police car. Abu handed me the card Brenda refused. "If you wake up in the night again and hear people talking, call us. Or if you see that stranger who drops his *g*s."

"I will." I watched them drive away. When I joined the others on the porch, Brenda was standing again. "They'll never find out what happened. Not with that Somali playing policeman. Damn immigrants."

Krista leaned across Rachel to face Brenda. "You mean damn immigrants or damn Black people?"

Brenda either forgot that Krista's was a mixed race family or she didn't care. "Whatever. Do what you want this morning. I'm going to paint." She slammed the door behind her.

"She's a bitch," said Krista.

Rachel had begun twisting her hair. "She's worse than when we were seniors. She knows more than she's saying. I wonder why she even invited us."

I moved Rachel's hand away from her hair. "Nostalgia. Loneliness. A whim."

Rachel corralled her hands in her pockets. "She could have made the whole thing up."

"But there were reservations in Hilton Head," Krista said, defending Brenda.

"She could have been lying about those. Made them herself then canceled them. All part of a plan to cover for her."

Krista asked what I didn't want answered. "Cover for what?"

Rachel reached for both our hands. "Her involvement. We need to be careful."

The door to Brenda's painting studio was open, so it hid the Calderwood crest that was emblazoned all around the house.

The visor turned down seemed to mask something terrible.

I knocked softly on the door frame, trying not to startle Brenda, who was focused on her painting. She looked up. "Deborah. You alone?"

"I am. Is there something you want to tell me?"

She dipped her brush into the red paint that was spread with other bright colors on her palette. "No. Just tired of being around people."

I came into the room and stood to the right of her. The quiet watercolors she used after she heard of Gerald's death were replaced with vibrant oils. The painting showed a collage of faces that looked like ours in elementary school. Rachel was at the bottom of the canvas, her hair bright red instead of black. Its length and blunt cut bangs were unmistakable. Overlaying her so one of her eyes was hidden, Krista was painted with her short hair blue and her glasses like the ones she started wearing in first grade. Brenda had painted me with oversized glasses and my hair in multitones of green. Our images were as distorted as our past, but we all looked happy.

"I like this. It brings back memories." I touched the blank space on the canvas. "Will your face go here?"

She ignored my question. "What do you want?"

"We're going to pick blueberries at the farm Esther told us about, then go to Damariscotta for lunch. You should come with us." I used a statement instead of a question.

"I just said I'm tired of being around people." She started the outline of her face.

"It's only us. We're friends."

"Still no. I'm going with Peter to arrange Gerald's funeral."

"Peter?" I couldn't disguise my surprise.

"Don't look so shocked. I asked him. He won't make judgments."

"I would have gone with you."

She added eyes to the painting. They looked lonely and distant from the other figures. "It's too late. "Go with your friends. Eat at The River Grill."

"We'll stop at a grocery store afterward. Get something to cook for dinner. Anything you want?"

"Whatever suits you." She started on the hair, gold and in the shape of coins, as if it were her money that separated her from us.

"There's one thing I don't understand."

"Only one?"

I ignored her sarcasm. "You invited us last September. Was Gerald lying to you even then about a golf trip?"

She stopped painting and held her brush toward me like a weapon. "Don't think too much."

I backed out of the room and closed the door. Eyes seemed to be staring at me from behind the visor on the crest.

CHAPTER 11

THE BLUEBERRY BUSHES stretched in rows toward one of Maine's numerous bays, the ocean air nourishing the hybrid varieties into berries twice the size of the wild ones. At a small table, a middle-aged woman who looked Somali was weighing the container of a white woman who'd filled it to overflowing.

"Guess Black people can work in the blueberry patches, but not in the police force," said Krista, softly enough that only Rachel and I heard.

Rachel put her hand on Krista's shoulder. "Give it a generation."

Krista brushed her hand away. "My kids can't wait."

I wanted to reassure Krista, to tell her that the Black Lives Matter movement was already making a difference. But even this wasn't going to change the resistance to Somali immigration in Maine. I wanted to believe that Brenda and Nelson's attitudes were not common, that Holland's tendency to overstep Abu wasn't because of racism but because he knew the people of Calderwood Cove.

The white woman handed the Black woman a twenty-dollar bill. Instead of accepting her change, she said, "Keep it. Your berries are the best around."

As the woman left, the woman in charge spoke with rolled *r*s and the careful enunciation that told me she was not a native speaker of English. "Wish they were my berries."

"Have they been all picked out?" I said. "We're pretty late to start."

"Go to the last two rows. There are only a couple of people there. Grab some of those milk jugs with the tops cut off that we use for buckets. Put one of the belts hanging next to them through the handle and strap the bucket to your waist. Makes the picking easier. You've got an hour before we close at eleven."

I'd picked plenty of berries, but never seen this system before. I'd remember it the next time I picked at the blueberry patch Rachel's sister-in-law still kept at the Cummings' farm in Shelby.

We each strapped one of the make-shift buckets around our waists and walked to the last two rows where berries clustered on the branches like a blue fireworks display. Grass and weeds grew unmowed between the bushes, wetting our sandals. I tasted a berry. It was sweet and deep, unlike the tart wild berries that made the best pies. I used my thumb and index finger to nudge some into my hand and dropped them into my bucket. Rachel and Krista talked beside me, their voices low as they remembered how we used to find patches of wild berries in the woods that surround Shelby's lake. I picked and listened, lulled into a kind of meditation until I became aware of a conversation in the row in front of me.

"I heard he was murdered." The voice was female with a New Jersey accent.

"Rob told me they found him smashed against the rocks at Pemiquid Light." This woman's accent was Boston Brahmin.

"Wouldn't surprise me if that wife of his killed him," said New Jersey.

"She's a snob, hardly talks to us. No reason she should be. She comes from some podunk town in New Hampshire. I think she married him for his money."

"Never mind money. I would have married him for his blue eyes. He was gorgeous." New Jersey's voice cracked.

Boston was quiet for a moment before she said, "Were you sleeping with him?"

"I wish. Let's go. You have enough berries?"

The two women stopped talking. I watched them pass the row we were in. The milk jugs hanging from belts looked comical on waists they must have kept teenager-trim in Pilates classes.

Rachel and Krista had both stopped picking. Rachel spoke first. "I think they're right. Brenda killed Gerald."

Krista started picking again. "Why would you think that?"

Rachel pulled clumps of berries off the branches, ignoring that she got half ripe ones mixed with the blues. "She doesn't care that he's dead. And there's that missing oyster shucking knife."

Krista stopped picking long enough to disagree. She wasn't ready to suspect a friend. "They're just jealous. I guess some people liked Gerald."

I began picking methodically, each berry and the women's conversation reminding me of Brenda's confession that Gerald's eyes had been as blue as Joseph Wheeler's.

"What's a midden?" I asked Krista, who was reading from a Damariscotta tourist brochure.

A waitress appeared with our check and answered for her. "It's a shell dump. We're not allowed to dump them now. It's a shell of what it once was." The sagging skin on the waitress's chin shook at the joke she'd made.

"It looks like we can walk there." Krista handed her credit card to the waitress and asked, "Is it worth a visit?"

The waitress took Rachel's credit card. "Brochure says it is. Whaleback Shell Midden. A National Historic Site. I haven't been there in years."

Krista closed the brochure. "It sounds more interesting than shopping for trinkets."

The waitress added the cash I handed her to the credit cards. "You should go to Renys. One of the stores is across the street. It sells clothing, mostly rugged stuff for hiking. Not my style. Renys Underground is what you want. It's next door. Not your usual trinkets. You can get everything from linens to camping gear to salt and pepper shakers in the shape of lobster claws." I watched her waddle away from our table with our payment. When she came back, we'd decided on a quick stop at Renys and a walk to the midden.

Outside, Damariscotta's Main Street greeted us with sidewalks full of tourists and rows of shops identified with so many oval signs I wondered if there was a town ordinance. Across the street the Maine Coast Book Shop announced itself with more oval signs below a green overhang. Above it, five arched windows lined the brick building. A sign hanging on the side of the building identified the space as the Lincoln Theater. It was streaming a Royal Ballet performance of *The Firebird*. Whatever the building had once been, it now served as the cultural center of Damariscotta. With the kind of telepathy we'd shared as kids, we forgot that we weren't interested in trinkets and turned right to the blue and white sign, this time rectangular, for Renys Underground.

The waitress wasn't exaggerating when she said we could get anything in the store. It could have been the original Walmart before that chain became homogenized with wide aisles and signage. Renys' clutter invited us to hunt for treasures. We were surrounded with tables of puzzles and coloring books and storage boxes and shelves of vases and figurines and garden trolls. We stopped at a display of kitchen goods. Set next to a rack filled with spices, we saw a selection of salt and pepper shakers tacky enough to add to the ones at Brenda's.

105

I picked up a set shaped like the state of New Hampshire. "I was going to get Brenda some like these on my way home. Should we add to her collection?"

Krista took them from me and put them back on the shelf. "It was Gerald's collection. Let's find her something else."

"I didn't come in here to buy a gift for Brenda. I'm going to browse. Meet me at the cash register in fifteen minutes." Rachel left us standing in front of an army of salt and pepper shakers.

Krista began looking through a rack of aprons. "Rachel's right. We should browse on our own. Don't worry about Brenda and Rachel. I'll keep the peace at dinner tonight."

"You always were the peacekeeper."

She held an apron that said "Mr. Good Lookin' Is Cookin." I shook my head no, cringing at the dropped *g*s. She put that one down and picked up another that said "Chef Ptomaine."

I nodded approval and found a table of puzzles. Rachel was at the end of that aisle in a section that held art supplies. I had just decided on a puzzle of sailing ships for my parents when a tall, thin man with red hair stopped at a table in front of mine. I clutched the puzzle against my chest as if it could protect me from him. When he saw me, he said, "Do you know if this Beast Feast barbecue sauce is good? It says somethin' about it being made for Maine's two hundredth anniversary."

I clenched my teeth at another dropped "g." "Who are you? Why are you hanging around Calderwood Cove?"

He set down the jar and looked closely at me. "You were on the beach."

"And you've been stopping in front of Brenda Calderwood's house. Are you related to Leroy O'Donnell?" Even at six feet away, I could smell marijuana on the flannel shirt he'd been wearing on the beach.

"Because we both have red hair?"

"That tells me you at least know him. Do you also know where he is?"

He picked up a package labeled Wicked Joe coffee. "Wish I did."

I set down the puzzle I'd been carrying and moved closer to the table where he was pawing through more jars of food and packages of candy. "What's your connection to the O'Donnells? They disappeared. Even the police can't find them."

"Why would the police want them?"

"They stole some things out of the shed," I seized on Brenda's lie. "Why do you want to find them?"

"None of your business." He set down a bag of Maine salt water taffy, picked up a jar of something from Stonewall Kitchen, and laughed. "This is even more Maine than the Beast Feast barbecue sauce."

"Brenda's my friend. She's my business. You called Gerald Calderwood last night and demanded money from her. Why? How's that connected to the O'Donnells?"

"Gerald who? I don't know what you're talking about."

"Did they kill Gerald?"

"Gerald's—" He caught himself. "You're telling me that someone named Gerald was murdered?"

"Don't act dumb. You called his house last night. I recognize your voice."

"If he's dead, there's nothin' I can tell you." He dropped the jar from Stonewall Kitchen. It shattered, spilling blueberry jam across the floor. He stepped over it and hurried to the door.

I bumped into a woman with a Renys shirt on, who was already calling for someone to clean up the mess. By the time I got outside, the man was disappearing on his bike down the side street next to the bookstore. I fumbled in my purse to find my phone and the card Abu had left me. All I could tell him was that the man couldn't have killed Gerald. He didn't know he was dead.

Whaleback Shell Midden was, as the waitress joked, a shell of what it once had been. Only small clumps of shells remained in the open fields and along the trails that the sign told us once contained mounds fifteen hundred feet wide and eight inches deep. Instead of what must have been permeated with flies and the smell of dead seafood, the area was green and free of the mosquitoes that would appear at sunset no matter how much the midden was sprayed. It felt good to be walking away from the pall of death that hung over Calderwood Cove.

Rachel stopped at one of the patches of shells. Ignoring the sign that cautioned us not to touch any, she picked up an oyster shell. "I had a friend who died from vibriosis."

Krista took the shell from her and tossed it away as if she were skipping a stone into the river that edged the midden. "From the bacteria?"

Rachel kicked at the shells and addressed me. "Krista knows about it. She's a biology teacher. You get vibriosis from eating raw bivalves. It's pretty rare. Most people just get sick. Oysters are a bigger business in New Orleans than Maine. Everyone knows the danger, but they still eat them raw."

Krista adjusted her glasses. She'd switched from the ones with the multishaded yellow frames she wore inside to the brown-gray ones that darkened in the sunlight. "Is that why you just picked at your oyster stew Friday night? Even though they were cooked, they reminded you of your friend?"

"I hadn't been thinking about him. He was actually more of an acquaintance. I don't like oysters." Rachel started walking away from the oyster pile. I knew she'd been thinking about

Joseph Wheeler that night. So had I.

We walked quietly along the path that was empty of the tourists who were crowding the Main Street sidewalk. When we reached the river, water was rushing under the bridge with the tide. We could see what the brochure identified as Glidden Midden on the other side. A connection hit me when I saw the higher mounds of shells. "Could Gerald have been poisoned with a raw oyster from Sproul's Oyster Farm and then stabbed with the oyster shucking knife?"

Krista stopped walking. "You called the police last night, didn't you?"

"I did. I talked with Scotty Holland."

Krista tamped down my speculations. "Wouldn't they tell you if he had vibrio in his system?"

"He only thanked me for the information. He's following Abu's caution. Not saying too much about the case."

Rachel agreed with me. "Deborah could be right about a deliberate poisoning. Oysters around here are farmed. They'd be checked before they go to market."

My head was spinning. I wanted to get away from oysters and shell dumps and redheaded men who made anonymous phone calls. "Let's go back. We can stop at that fish market we passed. Get something for dinner."

"Not oysters," said Rachel.

"Scallops," said Krista.

Another bivalve. "We'll cook them well," I said.

"We need to buy a vegetable to go with the scallops." Krista handed the package from the fish market to me. She reached into her purse for the brochure she'd put away.

"We passed a Hannaford's on the drive in." I moved the bag

of scallops from my left hand to my right away from my purse. "Maybe we should also buy some ice cream. There should be an ice cream parlor nearby."

Rachel dodged a splatter of guano in the middle of the sidewalk. "Not the grocery store kind. There was an ice cream stand close to Hannaford's."

Krista read from the brochure. "Round Top Ice Cream. It says here that it's on land that's been farmed for over two-hundred and fifty years. It was a dairy farm from 1922 to 1968. Now the land hosts a center for the arts in addition to selling the best ice cream in Maine. Looks like we can buy a hand-packed quart."

"Or two." Rachel rubbed her stomach. "Maybe by dinnertime I'll be able to think of food again."

We reached the downtown and my car where Krista and Rachel had left their purchases from Renys. Krista pointed to a sign beyond the store. "I guess that means we shouldn't stop at Waltz Soda Fountain."

Rachel and I groaned. When I got home, I'd go on a vegetable diet. I slowed down when I heard what sounded like the high screech of a bug across the street. A black Volkswagen was just being parallel parked. Peter and Brenda got out. I started to call to them when Krista grabbed my arm. "Leave them alone. They're making funeral arrangements. Who's she with?"

"Esther's tenant. Peter. He's a poet. This is nowhere near the funeral home." I watched them turn down a side street and enter a doorway on the corner. A window on the second floor announced Foster Law Office.

Krista saw what I was looking at. "Why would Brenda bring a poet to a law office?"

"And why would she lie to us?" I said.

CHAPTER 12

SOMETHING FELT DIFFERENT in the house. An emptiness I couldn't explain until I saw the dining room table. The salt and pepper shakers were gone. The collection on the hutch had disappeared. When we went into the kitchen, there were no more coffee mugs with the Calderwood crest.

I opened the refrigerator and unloaded the groceries. The bottles of white wine we'd brought for Brenda sat on one shelf and a pie sat alone on another.

Rachel stood behind me with two quarts of ice cream. "Looks like Esther's been busy. What kind of pie?"

I moved it to the front of the shelf so I could see beneath the lattice crust. "Cherry. I'm glad we bought vanilla ice cream."

"The maple walnut will be just as good." Rachel bent to put the ice cream in the freezer. "Ouch." She picked up a piece of glass she'd knelt on and dumped it into the trash can.

"Is there more glass in there?" I asked.

Rachel closed the lid. "No. The piece looked like it was from a mug. I wonder if Brenda broke one while she was putting them out of sight."

Krista surveyed the floor. "If she did, she swept up most of the pieces."

"And she emptied the trash can," said Rachel. "There's nothing in it except a new trash bag."

"That's odd," I said. "I emptied the can last night. There shouldn't have been much in it except coffee grounds and the bagel I didn't finish at breakfast."

Rachel opened the lid and pointed inside. "See for yourself. I wasn't lying." She slammed the lid back down.

Krista touched her arm. "We know you're not lying. Let's finish in here."

"I'll be right back." The emptied can bothered me. I went outside and found the bin by the shed. The top was tilted half on. I lifted it and saw the kitchen bag, its plastic ties pulled tight. I loosened them. Inside I saw mugs and salt and pepper shakers, all smashed. I put the lid on quickly as if hiding the destruction would block out my fear.

Inside, Rachel and Krista were looking around the living room. All the paintings Gerald had chosen were taken down. Nail holes punctured the walls. The set of Calderwood coasters on the coffee table were gone, the roses in the vase next to them dead.

"She's trashed everything," I said. "The bin outside was filled with broken mugs and salt and pepper shakers. She must have taken a hammer to everything breakable."

Krista moved toward the smaller sitting room. "She's getting rid of everything connected to Gerald. I hope she stopped at this part of the house."

It looked like she had. The cow in her painting of the barn stared down at us. Krista picked up the copy of *Wuthering Heights* that was in the same place I'd seen it when I first arrived. "It doesn't look like she's been reading this. There's no bookmark."

Rachel took the book from Krista and put it back on the table. "It's all about obsessed love. Ghostly, as I remember it."

The fog of Maine's coast reminded me of the fog on the moors in Brontë's novel and enveloped me in a memory that had been hanging over us all weekend. A barn, the dead body of Joseph Wheeler, the love for him that Rachel and Brenda both carried like an obsession. The windowless sitting room was as claustrophobic as Heathcliff's farmhouse. The door to the bedroom Brenda shared with Gerald was closed and I wondered if she had felt as trapped there as Catherine had been in her marriage to Edgar Linton. I knocked on the door, telling myself that she'd left her bedroom undisturbed and that she was resting there.

Rachel turned the doorknob. "She won't have gotten back before us." She opened the door and Krista and I followed her inside. A breeze and the smell of salt air was blowing through the window into the room. Another smell, of burned ashes, lurked beneath the freshness of the air. It came from a roasting pan on top of an armoire whose doors and drawers were open and empty.

Rachel tipped the pan. It held the remnants of burned papers. A half-burned photo of Gerald lay on the top. His face was covered in black marker. The bed was piled with pants, sport coats, enough shirts for half-a-dozen men. Lying on top were Gerald's golf shoes, grass-stained and slashed. When I looked closely, I could see knife slashes across some of the clothes. The knife was stuck into a tin replica of the Calderwood crest that hung crooked on the wall over the bed.

I felt a wave of repulsion in my groin. "She's not cleaning out, she's destroying." Brenda's anger wasn't like the anger I felt when Nathan and Cathy died and I was paralyzed for months before I found the energy to sort through their things.

"Should we call a doctor?" Krista's voice shook. "We can't leave her tomorrow if she's still like this. She could hurt herself."

"She won't. Whatever she's angry at, she's free of Gerald." Rachel sounded calm, only a brief touch of her hair showing her tension.

"Someone should stay longer than tomorrow. Until she's calm enough to be alone." I hoped Krista would volunteer.

"I can't," said Rachel. "I have to catch an early flight tomorrow."

I had seen the departure information on her itinerary. This time she wasn't lying.

"I can stay until tomorrow afternoon, then I have to get home. I have a meeting of our Conservation Commission at seven. I'd skip it, but we're drafting a proposal to buy a plot of land for a wildlife sanctuary." Krista's commitment didn't surprise me. She was still devoted to nature.

I spoke reluctantly. "I'll stay until Wednesday noon, but I have to be back for a program our library is hosting. I'll make sure Esther's here to check on Brenda. Maybe Peter as well."

We closed the door on Brenda's fury and climbed the stairs. At the end of the hallway, we could see that the door to the studio was open. Before we went into the room, I moved the door to see if the Calderwood crest still hung on it. It was gone, and in its place Brenda had hung the painting she'd been working on when we left. The image she'd painted of herself smiled down on the three of us.

"She looks happy," said Krista.

Rachel put her hand over Brenda's image then drew it away. "Not happy. Triumphant. Like she's controlling us."

Krista and Rachel were both right. Brenda looked like a cult leader overseeing her acolytes. I pushed the door against the wall so we didn't see the painting. "Isn't that what art does? Encourages interpretation."

Rachel went into the room first. "How do you interpret this?"

A box was pushed against the wall of the bedroom. I could see that it contained shorts and shirts, neatly folded. Her studio held none of the chaos of the bedroom she'd shared with Gerald. The bed was made, her paints were straightened, the brushes were washed and lined up in order of size. I pulled up the cloth that hung over the easel. The canvas was blank.

"It looks like she's ready to paint something else." Rachel picked up an open sketchbook that rested against the canvas. "This is good quality. Much better than any I saw at Renys."

She passed the sketchbook to Krista, who held it so we both could see. The lines were in pencil. They showed a view of the church in Shelby, the one that had been renovated into the library I now ran. Two figures faced front, a boy and a girl. They were holding hands. I couldn't tell if the girl's long hair would be strawberry blond like Brenda's or almost black like Rachel's, but I was sure that she'd paint the eyes on the boy blue like Joseph's.

Krista put the drawing back on the easel. "She's fixated on the past. That's not good. She needs to look forward."

"Don't worry about Brenda. She created her future. I'm going for a nap." Rachel pivoted from the easel and left Krista and me to interpret what she meant.

Krista stepped to the window. "Rachel thinks Brenda killed her husband. Do you?"

"It's because Rachel was worrying about Brenda even before she arrived. She came in on Wednesday and spent Thursday wandering around Portland."

"Why?"

"She said she wanted to prepare herself. Remember the tension between them our senior year?"

"I guess I blocked that out. We need to keep the peace between them." She acknowledged her role as peacekeeper again. "How can there be so much hate in such a beautiful setting?" Before I could answer, she said, "It's going to be a long night," and left the room.

I stood in front of the window, concentrating on breathing in the sea air. In the distance, I could just make out the ocean. The few houses visible before the road dipped toward the country club reminded me of the fairy houses we'd made as innocent kids. I wanted to go back to the grove on Monhegan Island when we still had a chance to enjoy the weekend. I wanted to take out the croquet set we'd put away before the storm and recall the simple rivalries of our childhood. We'd raked up the grass so it looked too perfect, a blanket covering the seething undercurrent that had invaded the house. I watched a hummingbird in the garden. It flitted among the flowers, its brisk motion like an electrical current pumping into my heart.

I sucked in a deep breath of the salty air and left Brenda's studio, keeping its door open so I wouldn't have to see her cult-like painting. I crossed the hallway and went into the room I'd been calling my own for the past four days. At first everything looked the same, even the towels I'd been using still impossibly white on the wooden rack. But the comforter on the bed was slightly rumpled as if something had been set on it and then picked up.

My suitcase was open, the way I'd left it. I rummaged through it to find a pair of socks and a long-sleeved shirt, convincing myself that I wanted these for a walk to the tiny beach, not that I was inspecting my suitcase to see that nothing was missing. Everything was there and the backpack that I'd rested beside it still had its zippers closed. I kicked my sandals under the bench and exchanged them for my sneakers. I sat on the bed to put on socks and shoes. That's when I noticed what was different in the room. The door to the armoire was slightly askew so the painted flowers on the front weren't flush. I jumped barefoot off the bed and opened the door. More of Brenda's clothes were shoved into the compartment. They were helter skelter, not neatly folded like the ones in the box in her studio. I pushed them in further and closed the door. It still stayed open a crack.

There were two drawers beneath the upper compartment. I opened each one. They were stuffed with clothes. I checked the three drawers in the bureau whose flower design matched the one on the armoire. The bottom drawer held Brenda's underwear, sexy bras and bikini panties, all silk and lace. The middle drawer was filled with nightgowns and matching robes. I realized that while the rest of us had been wearing flannel bathrobes and pajama bottoms topped with old T-shirts, Brenda had always emerged from her bedroom fully dressed. Why wasn't she flaunting the kind of sexy, expensive lingerie she bought with Gerald's money? Or he bought for her? If she wanted to cast it off the way she was casting him off, she wouldn't have carried it upstairs to this room.

I opened the top drawer. It held jewelry boxes and various containers of make-up. Tucked into one corner was a prescription bottle. It was the only thing I touched, so I could read the label. Lithobid. 300 MG Tabs. Take one tablet by mouth three times a day. I knew from a neighbor that Lithobid was a brand name for lithium. Brenda's behavior began to make sense. Even in high school she'd have bouts of energy and then would lapse into days of silence when we'd have to coax her out of her bedroom.

I closed the drawer and left my room to tell Rachel and Krista. This would help us understand Brenda's erratic behavior over Gerald's death. Rachel was lying on her bed asleep. I left her alone and went into Krista's room.

She was leaning against a pillow, a book propped in front of her on another pillow. When she saw me, she took off the orange-framed glasses she used for reading and put on the ones with the mottled yellow frame that she'd set on the bedside table. "What's up?"

"Move over. We need to talk."

She put her book on the table and scooched over to make

room. I'd forgotten to look in the drawer at my own bedside table, but I walked around the bed to look in hers. The only things inside were Krista's cell phone and three cases for the different glasses she wore. Unlike Rachel and Brenda, she'd never been glamorous, but I had to admire the statement her glasses made. Unique and energetic, the way she'd always been when we were growing up. I closed the drawer and went to the armoire. Krista watched me open the upper doors and the drawers and then move to the bureau.

"What are you doing? Only my dirty clothes are in the top drawer. The others are empty."

"Except this one." I lifted a large folder out of the bottom drawer.

"That wasn't there before. I was going to put clothes in the drawer but decided not to bother unpacking my suitcase."

I carried the folder to the bed and handed it to Krista while I settled myself next to her. She opened the folder. It held only one photograph. Brenda was sitting on a bed holding a baby. The back of the photo had a name crossed out so we couldn't read it. The date said July 16, 1998.

Krista closed the folder. I took it from her and looked again. "She's in her bedroom. That baby's a newborn. It must be hers."

"That's the year I got married. She couldn't come to my wedding because of her boyfriend. Gerald. The baby must be his."

"Why would she give birth at home? Do you think she kept it from him?"

Krista looked at the photo again. "There's a bigger question. Where's the baby now?"

"There's something else she's not telling us. Her clothes are all in my room, stuffed into the armoire and all the drawers."

"That makes sense. She's moving out of the room she shared with Gerald. You saw what she did to his clothes. She's angry."

"She's bi-polar."

Krista pushed herself straighter. "She's grieving. Sometimes she's angry, sometimes she's sad. It's normal."

"It's not. There's a prescription for lithium in one of the drawers."

Krista slid off the bed. She took the folder from me, put it into the bottom drawer, and came back to sit on the edge of the bed. I moved next to her.

"I knew that."

I stood up and faced her. "How long?"

"Just since we got her invitation. When I told my mother about it, she asked how Brenda was doing. We were neighbors, remember. Apparently she was diagnosed in high school. Remember how she acted back then? She was manic after Joseph died, then she closed herself off for nearly a month. My mother helped Brenda's mother find a doctor for her. Whatever medicine he gave her helped. Brenda was okay the rest of the year."

"Why didn't you tell Rachel and me?"

"I actually forgot about it. My mother said the medicine worked. There wasn't a need to tell you."

"If she came back to Shelby pregnant, your mother must have seen her and known."

"Maybe your mother knew, too. Shelby's a small town and we were all friends."

"We need to call them."

Krista got off the bed and went over to her window. "Why? It was a long time ago. Whatever happened, Brenda doesn't want us to know."

"She's not okay. Do you think she stopped taking her pills?"

"That would explain the clothes and all the pictures. It would take a lot of energy to do what she did. Is there a doctor listed on the medicine bottle? We can call if Brenda isn't calmer when she gets back."

"I'll check. I'll also go talk with Esther. She'll be able to tell us if Brenda has mood swings."

"Come talk to me after you see her." Krista kept her back to me.

I left her standing by the window. In the hallway, I could see into Rachel's room. She was still napping, so I went into mine to check the drawer by the bedside table. It was empty. I found the prescription bottle in the bureau and read the label. Dr. Adam Rush. The pharmacy was in Boston.

When I went to my suitcase to get my phone and plug in Rush's name, I looked out the side window at Esther's house. Nelson was standing next to a bicycle, holding out an envelope. The G-man. He'd taken off his flannel shirt and I could see his tattooed arm. Shamrocks. I ran downstairs. By the time I got outside, the bike had disappeared and Nelson was walking toward the parking area in the back of the house.

CHAPTER 13

"WAIT," I CALLED to Nelson when I came around the corner of his house. The door to his truck was open and he had one foot inside.

He took his foot out and faced me. "Where's the fire?" He pointed to my bare feet.

I ignored their burning. "You were talking to that man on a bike who keeps showing up. Who is he? I saw shamrock tattoos on his arm. Is he related to the O'Donnells?"

"Those tattoos weren't shamrocks." Nelson stepped into his truck, closed the door, and started the engine.

I grabbed hold of the door where the window was down. "You're lying."

"Go talk to my mother. She'll tell you who I was talking to. She's in the garden."

I jumped away as he backed the truck up. He left a tire track in the grass when he peeled out of the driveway. Peter hadn't found someone to help him clear the fallen tree branch. I climbed over it to reach Esther in her garden. She wore a straw hat with a wide brim and a loose-fitting dress that fell to her calves.

I snapped at her, my voice carrying the negative energy Nelson had stirred up. "Nelson was talking to that skinny guy on a bicycle."

Her green eyes snapped back at me. "Why are you so angry? Nelson doesn't know anything about him."

The envelope told me otherwise, but I didn't contradict her. "I think he's connected to the O'Donnells. He has tattoos. They looked like the ones Maureen has, but Nelson said they aren't shamrocks." Why hadn't I noticed the tattoos on his arm before? I pictured our conversation. The man's anorectic thinness had been concealed under a worn-out flannel shirt. Whatever else he was, he needed a job. Or the money he'd demanded from Brenda.

"I don't get this tattoo stuff. Maureen's shamrocks will look like seaweed when she's my age." Esther jiggled the flesh that sagged from her biceps. The Maine accent crept into her voice when she added, "Nelson doesn't know way-ah Maureen is."

"He knows something. He gave the man an envelope."

"I'll ask Nelson about it when he comes home."

"Did he come home from work early? Where'd he go now?"

"You're a suspicious one. Sometimes he comes home and goes back."

"Was he here to meet that guy? Give him something?"

"I never ask why he comes home, but he told me that man wants a job. Looks too decrepit to me to work at the oyster farm." She resumed her picking.

I calmed down enough to notice the garden. I could see where she'd pushed poles that had been knocked over by the storm back into the ground. Only a few bean shoots were broken off. Except for a toppled tomato plant, the rest of the garden had survived. Peas grew so high she had to stand on her toes to pick them. "In by Easter, pick by the Fourth of July." The saying was more than accurate. These vines were weighted down with peas to shell and sugar snap peas to eat whole. Cucumbers and squash had begun to flower. In a few weeks, Esther would be begging people to take a zucchini. The surviving tomato plants would top their cages and the basil underneath them would flourish. I always thought of gardening as a study in hope. Would white flies find the squash, aphids infest the kale, hornworms chew on the tomatoes? Esther seemed to have all those possibilities under control.

"Do you do this all yourself?" I said.

"Used to. Now I just do the harvesting. It's better to pick in the morning, but I was busy."

I thought back to the morning. Busy meant watching Holland and Abu at Brenda's. I didn't press her. "How do you fertilize to get such healthy plants?"

"Nelson sends someone from the oyster farm to get the soil ready. Whoever comes always tills in some crushed oyster shells. Good for the calcium. Peter's keeping it weeded this year. You have a garden?"

"Nothing like this. Much smaller. I just plant the basics. A few tomatoes and cucumbers, beans, one zucchini mound."

She pointed to a tomato plant beginning to flower. "You should try these. Lucid Gem. Black on top, shades of yellow and red on the bottom. Pretty to look at and even better to eat."

"Lucid Gem. I'll remember that for next year and hope they don't get attacked by hornworms. I'm always doing battle with bugs." I wanted to add, "And nasty men like Gerald and Nelson."

"Try companion planting. Carrots love tomatoes." She stood on her toes to get a few more peas that she dropped into a basket. "Can you carry that basket for me?" She pointed to the one with the snap peas. "When I start harvesting tomatoes and squash, I'll need a bigger basket. It'll get heavy, but Peter will help me."

She walked around the fallen branch toward the house before I could tell her about seeing him in Damariscotta and ask about Brenda's erratic behavior. I looked at Peter's door as I followed her inside. How had a young valet from Boston's Algonquin Club become someone Brenda trusted to take her to a lawyer after her husband died? Was he a friend more than a valet? Or more than a friend? Which of them needed the lawyer? Why?

I followed Esther through her back porch into her kitchen. She set a tin bowl on the table next to the basket of the peas that needed shelling. She started putting the snap peas from the other basket into a plastic container. "What's your dinner tonight? Want some of these peas?"

"Thanks, but we bought asparagus to go with the scallops we're having."

"Take some anyway. They're easier than asparagus. I hate peeling those stalks."

"You peel asparagus? I never heard of that."

"Just peel them so the stalks are more even. Cut off a little of the bottom. Not so much waste as snapping off the bottoms."

I trusted her but I couldn't imagine myself standing at a counter peeling asparagus. All the ends I snapped off went into my freezer with other vegetable scraps that I boiled down for broth. "Thanks for the tip. Maybe I'll try it tonight."

Esther had taken a plastic bag out of a drawer and was filling it with the sugar snaps. When the bag was three quarters full, she put it on the table next to the tin bowl along with the basket she'd emptied. "You can use these raw with whatever dipping sauce Brenda serves. She loves to lay out hors d'oeuvres. More time for her to drink wine before dinner."

"She does seem to drink a lot. Do you think she has a problem?"

"Who wouldn't, married to a man like Gerald. She'll be better now that he's dead."

"Maybe so, but doesn't it worry you that he was murdered?"

She moved a strand of hair that had fallen out of her bun and looked at me with her cold, green eyes. "Not really. Whoever killed him won't kill me. Won't kill Brenda either."

I pushed a perfect row of peas into the bowl. In the shell, they looked like little babies in an illustration I remembered from one of Cathy's picture books. Esther should worry that her own child could be a murderer.

"Actually, I came over to talk about Brenda, not about Gerald's death. "We think there's more going on with her than drinking."

Esther paused before she emptied the shell she'd opened. "Maybe she forgot her meds."

"You know about that?"

"Gerald told me that first summer they were married. She'd go wandering in the night talking to the trees. One morning I found her on my porch holding my cat and talking to him like he was a baby. Nelson took her home; Gerald took her to Boston. When they came back a month later, my cat was dead and Brenda was on some kind of medicine for manic depression."

"They call it bipolar now. I think she had it in high school."

"That's what Brenda told me. It started after some friend died."

"She takes lithium for it."

"Isn't that what makes batteries explode?"

I'd never made the connection. "It's a natural element, so I guess it has many uses."

"She called it the happy drug."

"It's a mood stabilizer. Has she had other episodes?"

Esther shelled another pea before she answered. "Last October. They'd gone to Boston for a few weeks and came back to close the house for the winter. She kept coming over and complaining about Gerald. I didn't think much about it. He's—was—controlling. Never even let her have her own credit card. I told her she could get her own. Even I have one. She said he'd find out because only he had a bank account."

"Right. She wouldn't be able to pay the charges. Maybe he was afraid she'd go crazy buying stuff if she was in a manic stage."

"Last October was the only other time I saw her like that. The night before they went back to Boston she was outside singing. Something about American pie. She has a beautiful voice."

I remembered that song. Brenda made us memorize the words. There were a lot of them. It took us the whole month of May before we graduated. She said it was about lost innocence. We'd harmonize the last line and change the "die" to "leave." It was an old song even in 1991, but I still felt sad when I heard it play on the radio. "It's a nice song. The pie's a metaphor for America."

"I know that. It's as American as apple pie."

"Right. Speaking of pie, will you join us for a piece of the cherry one you made?"

"Don't mind if I do." Esther's pie making was more about us and what we might know than the joy of baking.

I pressed her. If Brenda's breakdown happened last October, she'd already sent us the invitations to visit. "Did she say anything about Gerald going on a trip?"

She shelled the last pod. Instead of putting the peas in the bowl, she put them into her mouth. "Now that you mention it, she did. That's why she was complaining about money. He was going away and she was worried about being alone."

"Was she afraid to be alone?"

"I don't think so. It was the money she kept talking about. I told her not to worry. I wasn't going anywhere. She wouldn't starve. When they came back on Memorial Day, she was fine. I'm glad you're here. Peter will help her but it's always good to have a woman around."

"We saw her with Peter in Damariscotta. Are they close?"

"She used to come over and play cribbage with me while Gerald was on the golf course. Lately, she cuts our time short and visits with Peter."

"He's at least twenty years younger than Brenda, isn't he?"

"They're not sleeping together if that's what you're implying." Esther curled her sunken chest forward in the kind of flirtatious movement I'd noticed before.

I wasn't suggesting anything, but this wouldn't be the first older woman-younger man affair I knew about. "I'm just wondering why she would say they were going to the funeral home. When we saw them in Damariscotta, they were going into a building with a sign for Foster's Law Office."

"Maybe she was helping Peter with a book contract."

"Has he written that many poems? Didn't you tell me you'd never seen any of them?"

Outside, a group of teenagers were singing about an old town road. It was as poetic as an imagined book contract. "Even if Peter had a book contract, he wouldn't need a lawyer. It's more likely that Brenda needs the lawyer."

"I suppose. Don't know why, though." Esther began filling freezer bags with the peas we'd shelled. If she knew anything, she wasn't going to tell me.

"It wasn't only Brenda and Peter that we saw."

She zipped one of the bags closed. "Who?"

"The red-haired guy Gerald was just talking to. He doesn't know Gerald is dead."

"I'll tell Nelson." She tipped the bowl to put the last of the peas into a bag.

I thanked her for the peas and left her still sitting at the kitchen table. Some of the phlox on Brenda's walkway had been torn up. I heard something behind the shed. The flower culprit. A cat, with a mouse hanging from its mouth. I closed the lid to the garbage can earlier, but it was half off and crooked again. I tried to straighten it so some nocturnal animal wouldn't get at it. There was no food inside to attract one. Only shards of glass from the smashed coffee mugs and scatterings of salt and pepper from the emptied shakers. I secured the lid and walked to the door, hoping that Brenda had expended all her energy when she destroyed Gerald's things.

I went onto Brenda's porch to call Abu. I sat with the cell phone in my hand, looking at the horizon and the sliver of ocean. High puffy clouds floated toward it, forming shapes like the ones we used to name when we were kids. I saw a lion's face, an owl, a church steeple. A gull crossed beneath a cloud that looked like a fish and dove toward the water for the real fish it spotted.

I found Abu's number from the last call I'd made and hit the call icon. He picked up quickly. "Deborah." He'd put my number into his contacts. "Have you more information?"

"Only about the man I saw in Damariscotta. He was on his bicycle talking with Nelson Sproul. Esther thinks he was asking Nelson for a job. I saw Nelson give him an envelope, so I think there's something else going on."

"We'll check with Nelson. Anything else?"

"Just one more thing." Abu didn't need to know about Brenda's personal life. "He had shamrock tattoos on his arm."

"I don't understand. Why's that important?"

"Nelson says they aren't shamrocks but I think he's lying. They looked like the tattoos Maureen O'Donnell has."

"Good to know. Thanks." He hung up before I did.

I began watching the cloud shapes again. Voices from the beach club drifted through the air. I looked at my watch. Four o'clock. Happy Hour. Rachel and Krista opened the door to the porch.

"Studying castles in the air?" Rachel used a line from *Little Women*.

I remembered Esther talking about the novel's croquet scene.

"I guess *Little Women's* the theme for the weekend."

Krista sat down in the chair next to mine. "Weren't the four girls dreaming about their futures in that chapter? Too late for us."

Rachel took the chair on my other side. "If we're the four little women, who's who?"

"You'd be Amy the artist and Krista would be Meg the motherly type." I pointed to the clouds. "I wasn't imagining castles. I was just watching cloud shapes."

"You know there's a word for seeing shapes in things," said Krista. "Pareidolia. Remember how we used to watch the clouds from your back yard? Rachel always had the best imagination."

"That's why she's Amy the artist." I pointed to the cloud closest to us. "What's that one look like?"

Krista said "a horse" at the same time that Rachel said "a unicorn."

Rachel turned to me. "I suppose you get to be Jo."

I laughed. "We're all *Jos*. Strong women."

"What about Brenda? She's selfish like Amy." Rachel pulled her knees onto the chair and wrapped her arms around them.

"And sick like Beth." said Krista.

Rachel hugged her knees. "What do you mean?"

Krista took off her glasses and stared at the horizon before she put them back on. "Without my glasses on, Calderwood Cove looks like the insanity in a Van Gogh painting. Brenda's troubled, but she's not really like Beth. She's too angry. Beth looked death in the face and accepted it."

"I still don't understand," said Rachel.

Krista spoke to me. "Tell her what you found."

"Krista's mother told her a couple of weeks ago. Brenda's bipolar. She started on medicine our senior year."

"We all could have used medicine then." Rachel's hand shot to her hair then came down again. Brenda might not have learned control, but Rachel had.

"She's still on it," I said. "I found lithium in a drawer in my room. While you were both resting, I went over to see Esther. She knows about the lithium. Brenda had an episode last October. It must have been around the time she sent us the invitations."

Rachel set her feet back on the porch floor. "Did Esther say how Brenda knew Gerald would be away?"

"No. But Esther made me think of something else. Gerald might not be as bad as we imagine. Those women in the blueberry patch liked him. He might have monitored Brenda's access to money so she wouldn't go on a crazy spending spree."

"I wouldn't go that far." Rachel pointed to one of the rocks that lay at the edge of the garden. "Never mind the clouds. Look at that face in the rock. That's what I imagine Gerald looks like."

Krista adjusted her glasses. "I don't see any face."

Rachel leaned toward me. "Deborah won't see it either. You need the right angle. It's mostly just the top of a face. I imagine that's what the eyes would look like beneath that visor on the Calderwood crest. Savage. Esther didn't like Gerald. Did she say anything else about him?"

"There was something more important than Gerald's character." I told them about the bicycle and the tattooed arm and the envelope. "Esther said he's looking for a job at the oyster farm."

"Did you believe her?" said Krista.

"I believe that's what she thinks. Like you said, Esther didn't like Gerald. She thinks Nelson knew something bad about him. Last Sunday, she saw Nelson throw an envelope at Gerald."

"So that's two envelopes?" said Rachel.

"Yes. Gerald tore that one up. Now Nelson's talking to someone with tattoos like Maureen's and the same coloring as

Leroy. Esther is suspicious enough that yesterday she wanted me to hack into Nelson's email."

"Did you?" Rachel looked at me as if I were a computer wizard.

"No chance of figuring out his password. But everything's connected somehow."

Krista got out of her chair, faced the ocean, then turned back to us. "There's one other thing. Deborah, tell her what else we found while she was sleeping."

I inched my chair closer to Rachel's. "We found a photo. Brenda was holding a baby. She was in her bedroom in Shelby."

Rachel reached for her hair. "She had a baby?"

"We think so. Krista's mother knew about the lithium. If Brenda had a baby at home, she must have seen her pregnant. They lived next door to each other."

Rachel grabbed my hand. "Shelby's a small town. Wouldn't lots of people have seen her?"

"It was 1998. The year of my wedding that none of you came to." Krista reminded us of the year we were all in our mid-twenties. "She could have stayed inside in her yard. Remember how high her fence was?"

"I'm sorry about your wedding," said Rachel. "I was in Europe. Deborah was pregnant if I recall. If Brenda's excuse was staying with a boyfriend in Maine, the baby must be Gerald's."

Krista left the railing. "I'll call my mother. My phone's upstairs."

"Use mine." Rachel gave Krista her phone. She went inside to make the call.

We waited in silence. I thought of my dead Cathy. Whatever happened to that baby Brenda was holding, I wanted to believe it was still alive.

It felt like a long time before Krista came back to the porch. She looked disturbed, even fearful. "We were right," she said. "Brenda had that baby at home. She kept it for just a day before she gave it up for adoption. My mother said she wouldn't tell anyone who the father was."

"Did your mother say if it was a boy or a girl?" I looked up as soon as I said this.

Brenda was standing in the doorway. "If who was a boy or a girl?"

CHAPTER 14

"YOUR BABY," RACHEL blurted out. "We found the photo." Brenda moved one of the Adirondack chairs so it faced Rachel and me and sat down. "I thought it would be safe in Krista's room. She's too nice to look through other people's drawers. I guess I was wrong."

Krista gave Rachel her phone before she sat down. She rubbed her hand on her pants as if she were wiping away dirt. She started to speak but stopped when Rachel taunted Brenda. "We're in your guest rooms. Guests assume drawers are for them."

"If you're in a hotel." Brenda reached toward the coffee table, ready to pour wine that wasn't there. "I suppose you found all the clothes I put in your room, Deborah."

I took hold of Brenda's hand, hoping to keep the tension from erupting into an argument. I thought her tremor was worse. Or maybe I noticed it more because we knew about the lithium. "Krista and I found the photo and the bottle of lithium. We told Rachel. She didn't open any drawers. Did you stop taking the medicine? Is that why you savaged all of Gerald's things?"

"The doctors say I'm bipolar."

"My mother told me," said Krista.

"So much for a confidence." Brenda directed her anger toward her as much as toward Rachel.

Krista held up her hand in a gesture meant to say hold on. "She only told me just before we came here. She kept your confidence for twenty-five years. She wondered how you're doing."

"Fine until my husband was murdered. I forgot to take my pills yesterday. Not to worry. I took one before I went to the funeral home. In case you're wondering, lithium is why my hand shakes. I can stop the tremors if I concentrate. She reached toward the table again. This time her hand was steadier.

Rachel challenged her. She was becoming more short-tempered, even nasty. "You were in Damariscotta with Peter. Nowhere near the funeral home."

A motorcycle speeding by muffled the beginning of Brenda's response so I only caught "a lawyer. Funeral's Wednesday at five, by the way. At the Beach Club. You'll all be gone and won't have to watch me play the grieving widow. But Wednesday morning I can take you to the Calderwood cemetery plot. It's quite a site for the five pounds of ashes I'll have from Gerald."

"I'll be gone early tomorrow," Rachel reminded her. "I can't change my plane reservation." She mouthed "Thank God" to me.

I had her itinerary memorized. Tuesday, July 6. 8:28 AM.

"I'm sorry. I need to leave Maine by noon tomorrow." Krista sounded more sympathetic than Rachel. "Deborah said she'll stay until Wednesday morning."

Rachel leaned toward Brenda, her posture confrontational. "Why did Peter go with you to a lawyer? Does it have something to do with your baby?"

"The lawyer's not your business. It's cocktail hour. I'll tell you about the baby after I've had a glass of wine. Deborah, help me in the kitchen." It was a command, not a request.

When we got inside, she said, "I need to get away from Rachel. Krista can calm her down."

"The four of us being together has brought back memories of

that last awful year in high school."

"She should get over it. She only lost a boyfriend. I've lost a husband."

"So did I."

Neither of us said anything else until she opened the refrigerator for the wine. She picked up the bag of peas. "What are these?"

"I helped Esther shell peas. She gave me some of these sugar snaps for our cocktail hour."

Brenda pushed me aside and began looking through the refrigerator. "I think I have some hummus. Find a bowl and wash the peas."

I opened a cabinet and took out a bowl that looked like it was the right size. I recognized it as the mosaic one her mother used to serve us fruit. "You have your mother's bowl. I loved this one. Whenever she took it out, I knew we'd have grapes or cherries or cut-up watermelon."

Brenda put a bottle of wine, a container of hummus, and three packages of cheese on the counter. "This will do."

"I ate some of the peas while I was helping Esther. They'd be great even without the hummus."

She opened another cabinet, took down a box of crackers, and dumped the crackers into a wicker basket. "Why were you at Esther's?"

"I saw Nelson talking with that guy on a bicycle."

"What guy on a bicycle?" Either she knew who I was talking about or didn't care because she opened the refrigerator and pointed to the pie. "Esther gave us this so she'll have an excuse to join us tonight and nose around some more."

"I thought you liked Esther."

"She's an old lady. She can be annoying." She found a corkscrew then threw it back into the drawer. "Screw top." She didn't approve.

135

I finished rinsing the peas and put them into the bowl. "Did you want to tell me something?"

"Like what?"

"I don't know. You asked me, not the others, to help in the kitchen."

"Like I said, I needed to get away from Rachel. You're also the only one who's met Peter. I'd like to know what you told the others about him."

I found a spot on the tray for the bowl of peas. "We all saw him in Damariscotta. I don't know anything to tell except that he's a poet."

"And young and good looking with those different color eyes. He's not my lover, if that's what you're thinking." Esther had said the same thing.

"He's way too young for that."

"If I tell you about something we've been planning, will you promise not the tell the others?"

"Planning what?"

"Promise."

"Okay, I promise."

"We've been planning an artists' retreat. Gerald didn't like it here, so we were going to approach him about turning the cottage into an artists' residence. We could get rid of the O'Donnells, Peter could stay in Esther's apartment and be the caretaker. Gerald could spend more time in Boston."

"What did Gerald think of the idea?"

"We never told him. Now that he's dead we can go ahead with our plans. That's why we went to see Leo Foster. He's going to do some legal work so Peter and I will be co-owners of the property."

"It's too soon. You hardly know Peter."

"I trust him." She lay a cutting board on the counter, unwrapped the cheese, and set the basket of crackers next to it. She reached for a knife in the wooden holder. The slot was empty. I shivered at the thought that the missing knife had killed Gerald and that she and Peter had planned an easier way to open a retreat than to convince him to accept the idea.

She took another knife. "This one will do," she said as she set it next to the cheese. She handed the cutting board to me and picked up the tray. I followed her onto the porch, pushing away a suspicion I couldn't believe.

Rachel and Krista were standing at the railing. They stopped whatever they were saying to each other when they heard us.

"The baby?" said Rachel.

"Sit down. I need a glass of wine first." Brenda held the bottle.

We sat and waited for her to open it. After she emptied all the wine into four glasses, she tasted hers. She set her glass down and read the label on the bottle. "King Estate Pinot Gris. From Oregon. I never heard of it, but it's good." She picked up her glass and swallowed more.

Rachel swirled her wine in her glass. "We're waiting."

Brenda tried to pour herself more wine. "Empty. I'll get us another bottle."

"Are you allowed to drink with lithium?" Krista hadn't tasted her wine yet.

"It's not a problem. I'll be right back." Brenda picked up the empty bottle and went into the house.

Rachel cut slices of cheese then drove the knife point into the cutting board. The sound broke the quiet of the late afternoon. Krista pulled out the knife and lay it on its side. "Relax, Rachel. Brenda will be okay now."

Rachel looked at the wine she'd barely tasted. "She drinks too much."

I motioned to the food on the table. "We need to see that she eats. Keep her from getting drunk."

"Us, too." Krista took a piece of the cheese that Rachel had cut.

I passed around the bowl of snap peas. "Esther knows how to garden. These are delicious. Don't drown them in so much hummus you can't appreciate them."

Krista held the cheese in her hand and looked at Rachel. "I need to ask you something. When I was phoning—"

She was interrupted when Brenda opened the door, slamming it behind her and setting a bottle she'd already opened on the table. Hers was the only empty glass. She sat down, filled it, and leaned back in her chair. "I'm ready to talk now. It doesn't matter. Gerald's dead and he'll never find out."

"You had a baby," said Krista. "My mother knew it. She only told me when I called her before you came back from Damariscotta."

"Your mother was a good neighbor. She helped me find a lawyer to arrange the adoption."

"It's hard to lose a baby," said Rachel, her voice low and sad and no longer confrontational.

"I couldn't keep him." Brenda set her wine glass on the table. "He was Gerald's, but Gerald was always clear that he wanted no children. He never knew. I thought about having an abortion. My parents found out I was pregnant and talked me out of it. They sheltered me and kept my secret. They would have helped me raise the baby. I had to choose. I chose Gerald. It was a mistake." Her sentences were clipped, her anger replaced with regret.

The cloud I'd been studying broke apart while she told her story. Her eyes were watery and brown. I remembered our biology class and our section on genetics when we all checked the color of our parents' eyes. Brenda's child would likely have the dominant gene, brown eyes, despite the blue of Gerald's she seemed to have fallen in love with. Or pretended to fall in love. "There are adoption records. You could find him."

"It's too late. I'm rid of Gerald. I don't need a child. I'm free now. I'll have more money than any of you. I'll be happy." She picked up her wine glass and added as she went into the house, "Again."

Krista stood up. She wasn't tall but looking down at Rachel and me sitting, she was imposing. All her athleticism permeated her rigid body.

"Something else is wrong," I said. "You look furious."

"Your phone, Rachel." She reached for the phone that was still on the table.

"What's the matter with my phone?"

Krista fiddled with some buttons and handed it to me. I sucked in a gasp when I saw it. I calmed enough to give it to Rachel. "Gerald Calderwood's phone contact. Why?"

Rachel studied her phone as if she had never seen the contact before. She waited a moment before putting it back on the table. "I'd forgotten."

"Forgotten? Like you forgot to tell us you came early to Maine?" A year and a half ago, Rachel had become a better friend than we were even thirty years ago. What had happened to her?

"After I was in Shelby, after we found out what happened to Joseph—"

"Wait a minute," said Krista. "You found out what happened to Joseph Wheeler?"

"Never mind that," I said. "We can't tell you. Can't tell anyone."

Krista looked like she wanted to argue. I held my hand up to stop her and confronted Rachel. "How does your being in Shelby explain Gerald Calderwood? He has no connection to the town."

"He does. I thought I might move back, so I checked out real estate. There's a plot of land at the base of the hill where we used to ski."

An image of Krista on the T-bar flashed before me. We always rode together because we were the short ones. Rachel and Brenda would pair up in front of us or behind us. Rachel's brother and Joseph Wheeler would tease us with jokes about the Mutts on one T-bar and the Jeff's on the other. "The ski area closed years ago. Even snowmaking got unreliable in our warming climate. Artists come in during the summer now. They create art out of natural objects they find in the woods surrounding the overgrown ski trails." I wanted to tell them about Brenda and Peter's plans, but I promised I wouldn't.

"I know," said Rachel. "I saw some of the art on-line when I was looking for property. There was one piece of land for sale. In the end, I couldn't bring myself to return to Shelby."

"What's that got to do with Gerald Calderwood?" Krista was still looking down on us.

"Either he owns it or he was selling it for Brenda's parents." Rachel looked at her phone. "I didn't recognize the name when I contacted him. It was before Brenda sent us those invitations for this weekend. I wish I'd never come."

"Why would one of them own land in Shelby?" I asked.

Krista sat down. "I remember. When Brenda's dad would pick us up from skiing, he always pointed to a section on the base of the hill. He'd say, 'I own that. Some day I'll sell it so they can build a new lodge.'"

I pushed my chair back and faced Rachel. "You should have remembered when Brenda invited us. You should have told us when you got to Maine." I went to the door and called back, "You both can clean up. I'll see you at dinner."

Maybe by then I could reconcile myself to Rachel's forgetting to tell us about her early plane flight and her contact with Gerald Calderwood. And forget about Brenda being financially involved with Peter.

CHAPTER 15

RACHEL HELD A forked scallop toward Brenda. "Well-cooked and delicious. We won't get vibriosis."

Brenda bit into an asparagus spear. We'd peeled the asparagus, laughing at the process. It relieved the tension that had built on the porch. Brenda chewed and drank wine poured from our third bottle. "Vibriosis. What's that?"

Rachel finished chewing her scallop. "Vibriosis. You should know that. You live in oyster country. People can get it from eating a raw oyster. Sometimes they die from it."

"Is that why there's a warning in all the restaurants about eating raw shellfish?" Brenda put a scallop into her mouth.

"Enough about vibriosis." Krista was cutting her asparagus into small bites. "This is a perfect meal. Just enough after our Happy Hour and before our pie. Esther will be over soon."

From where I was sitting I could see a flashing blue light coming down the street. "Something must have happened. Maybe at the Beach Club?" When the flashing light stopped in front of Esther's house, I jumped up. "Do you think something happened to Esther?"

Brenda reached for the bottle of wine. "You can check."

I went out the back door, thinking about Brenda sitting calmly in her chair eating and drinking. Esther was her friend, not mine, though I was starting to count her as one of the old women I admired. She reminded me of Bertha, who used to be librarian in Shelby and came faithfully to the library every week. I wondered about my affinity for women like them. Maybe because they seemed to live in a simpler time, though I'd learned that Bertha's life in Shelby had been far from simple. Maybe Esther had a darkness in her past that she'd survived.

I watched Holland and Abu get out of a white and blue state police car. I was afraid that an ambulance would appear behind it. Esther came to the door. She saw me and motioned me over.

Krista came out of Brenda's house and was about to follow me until Esther called out, "Just Deborah. Whatever it is, I'll tell you all when I come for pie." She waited until I stepped onto the porch to let Holland and Abu inside.

Her voice was steady when she said. "What is it? Something about that red-haired man Nelson was talking to?"

"It's about Nelson," said Holland.

Esther's green eyes glowed under the overhead light and fan she switched on when we came into the sitting room. I thought of my biology class again. Only two percent had green eyes. Odd how that genetics lesson stuck with me. Maybe because I remembered reading about eye color in a Trixie Belden novel when I was in third grade.

The fan squeaked. "Fan needs an adjustment," said Holland.

"Nelson will fix it."

"Sit down, Esther." Holland motioned her to a sofa that faced the front window. Through it I could see Krista going back into the house.

Esther grabbed my hand and pulled me onto the sofa next to her. Holland and Abu towered above us.

"Don't just stand there, Scotty." She still held my hand. Hers felt frail, not like the strong hand she gardened with. "Say what

142

you have to say."

Holland sat on the only chair in the room, his blue uniform shirt blending into the blue fabric of the chair's upholstery. He looked like he belonged there. "Get yourself one of those dining room chairs." He motioned Abu to where we'd shared tea and pie with Esther four nights ago.

Abu returned and placed the chair so he could look directly at Esther. "Nelson's at the station in Wiscasset. We're questioning him about fraud at Sproul's Oyster Farm."

Esther released my hand and waved a bony finger at Abu. "Shh. Scotty will tell me what's happened."

Holland glanced at Abu, who nodded to tell him okay. "Someone at Sproul's is selling oysters to a fake client who never gets billed. The client sells the oysters and funnels the money back to someone at Sproul's."

Esther sat as straight as her crooked body allowed before she spoke. "Why's that a crime? What difference does that make? As long as Nelson gets paid."

"Thousands of oysters are unaccounted for," said Holland. "No paperwork involved. No taxes. Money into someone's pocket. Explain the rest, Bashiir."

Abu's arms fell to the side of the straight-backed chair. He looked uncomfortable. "It's an ongoing investigation. All I can tell you is what we told Nelson. Whoever is involved at Sproul's sells oysters illegally through a middle man. Oysters flood the market and the prices drop, but Sproul's has already unloaded what was ready for market."

"I can't he-ah him, Scotty. His accent's too strong. Tell me what he said." Esther fell into her Maine accent as if to tell Abu he was an outsider.

Holland explained again.

Esther leaned closer to me. "Nelson wouldn't do that. Why

would you even be looking at his oyster business?"

"We've known for a year that someone was flooding the oyster market. We checked all the oyster farms looking for a connection to Gerald Calderwood's murder."

Esther jumped up. As frail as she seemed, she was still agile. "Are you accusing my son of fraud?"

"The fraud came from his farm. Nelson double profited. He sold more oysters than any other farm and evaded taxes. We need to search his room and bring his computer to the station. We have a warrant." Abu showed Esther the warrant.

She spoke only to Holland. "You know me, Scotty. You don't need a warrant."

Abu kept hold of the warrant as they left the room. Esther sat down and dropped her head to her chest, her back curving into her dowager's hump. When she lifted her head, her green eyes flashed a suspicion her words didn't. "Nelson's not guilty." "I hope not. But there has to be a connection to Gerald's murder. You need to tell the police about the envelope Nelson gave to him. I told Abu about the one he gave to the man on the bicycle." "You should have let me tell Scotty." She stood up again and pressed against me, her tiny body lost under the pink lounge suit she'd worn the day I met her. Instead of a strong, elderly woman, she felt worn down and afraid. "Nelson will explain those envelopes."

Holland and Abu came into the room, Holland carrying a folder of papers and Abu holding Gerald's computer.

Esther planted herself in front of Holland. "I'm coming with you. Nelson will bring me home."

Abu looked down at her. "No. You need to stay here. Nelson claims he's innocent. He doesn't know why thousands of oysters aren't accounted for. We're only questioning him. Even if we find reason to arraign him, we'll release him tonight."

"I'll wait with you," I said.

"Thank you," she murmured.

We watched at the window until Holland and Abu drove away. Across the street, I could see a raccoon heading toward Brenda's trash can. I hoped it would cut its feet on any glass I'd missed from the broken Calderwood mugs.

When the car pulled away, I faced Esther. "I need to ask you something."

She sank into the sofa while I stood looking down on her. "Don't just stand there. Ask what you need to."

"Why did you want to look at Nelson's computer? You know something."

"I know the oyster farm's in trouble. I wanted to see the numbers. There might be a way I can help."

"Does it connect to Gerald? Is that why they had a fight?"

Esther sank further into the sofa. "I never should have told you that. I have no idea what was in the envelope. Go put more clothes on. It's going to be a long night."

I waited in the chair Holland had sat in, lulled by the squeaking fan and the copy of *Moby-Dick* I'd brought back from Brenda's when I walked across the street in my bare feet to tell her and the others what was happening. My sweater and the socks and sneakers warmed me.

Esther was dozing on the sofa, snoring softly through her open mouth. When Nelson's truck turned to the back of the house, she snapped her head up so fast I feared she injured her neck. I went over to her so she wouldn't stand half-awake. She held onto my arm until she got her balance. "You can go now."

"I'll wait. Nelson can tell both of us what's going on."

"He won't like that. Go home."

I wanted to say that home was four hours away in New Hampshire. I'd had enough of Calderwoods and Sprouls and fraudulent oysters. Esther opened her door and shooed me out as if I'd been an invading mouse. Behind the house, I could hear Nelson and Peter talking in muffled voices. If Peter had been home all night, I wished he had checked on Esther.

I stopped, trying to hear what they said. Nelson's voice came through angrily. "Oyster fraud's the least of it. They found vibrio bacteria in Gerald's tox screen."

Peter said something I couldn't make out, but I could hear Gerald's response. "Vibriosis wasn't enough to kill him. It made him sick and a knife finished him off. I'm afraid they'll be accusing me of murder."

They stopped talking and Nelson came around the corner. He saw me and yelled, "Get the hell home."

I got to the street as fast as I could, a thousand suspicions running through my head. Rachel knowledgeable about vibriosis because of a friend's death. Krista knowing about it because of her background in biology. Brenda pretending ignorance about the danger of eating shellfish. Nelson's oyster fraud. His tone and his possible connection to Gerald's murder frightened me. Fog had rolled in from the ocean, so thick the light on Brenda's back door was only a pinprick. The moist air coated my face and filled my lungs. Nothing stirred, not even the animals that haunted Brenda's trash cans.

The door didn't open. I pressed harder on the handle. It was locked. Had everyone forgotten that I'd be coming back when Nelson returned? I fumbled in the dark for a likely place to find a key. Under the doormat, under one of the rocks at the side of the path, on the arm that attached the light to the house, all the spots were empty.

I walked to the side. No light shone in any of the windows.

I continued to the porch steps, ignoring the water that was seeping from the grass into my sneakers. All I could see were eerie shapes made by the drifting fog. I found the railing to the porch steps and climbed them. If the door was locked, I'd sleep on the lounge and cover myself in pillows from the Adirondack chairs. I tripped on something at the top of the steps. Whatever it was tumbled down, echoing in the silence of the night.

I found my way to the door and held my breath as I pressed on the handle. I pushed on the door, hard, and breathed out when it opened. No one had left a light on for me. I felt my way to the back door where I remembered there was a light switch. When I flicked it on, it illuminated the dining room table and half of the cherry pie. A note lay next to it in Rachel's handwriting. "I'm leaving at 5:00. I'll wake you to say goodbye."

Exhausted, I left the light on and the pie untouched as I climbed the stairs to my bedroom.

CHAPTER 16

"**D**EBORAH. I'M LEAVING." Rachel's whisper blended with the knife that was peeling asparagus in my dream. I opened my eyes to her blurred face.

She handed me the glasses on my night stand and turned on the light. I blinked against the glare then pushed myself up and moved to the edge of the bed. My feet dangled to the floor that felt cold under them.

Rachel sat next to me. "Did you talk with Nelson? Find out anything else?"

"Esther wouldn't let me stay, but I heard him talking with Peter. Gerald had vibriosis."

"So he died from eating an oyster? No murder after all?"

"There was a stab wound so there was a murder. Oysters from around here are pretty clean. I'm guessing he was also poisoned."

"Get yourself back to Shelby. Don't eat any shellfish."

"I promised another day. Then I'll leave. There's something else. When I got back here, the door was locked. Why didn't you leave it open and leave some light on? The fog was so thick I had to feel my way to the front."

"I was the last one in bed. I checked that both doors were unlocked and left the lights on."

Cold traveled from my shoulders through my stomach and

into my already cold feet. "Brenda locked me out on purpose."

"She was sleeping when I came upstairs."

"She must have woken up. Unless someone else came inside." I tried to remember if Nelson had stopped his truck before I heard him talking with Peter. He could have come into Brenda's house first.

The grandfather clock at the bottom of the stairs struck five. Rachel hugged me and stood up. "I'll call when I'm in New Orleans."

We went into the hallway and saw that Brenda's door was still closed. Krista's was open. She heard us and called out, "Wait a sec." She came into the hall to say goodbye. "As awful as this weekend has been, I'm glad I saw you again. We all seemed as close as when we were kids. Let's stay in touch."

Even at dawn, Krista could be positive. Despite her knowledge of vibrio bacteria, I realized that she was almost the only person I didn't suspect of murder.

Without embracing Krista, Rachel lifted her suitcase to carry it downstairs. "Yes, let's stay in touch."

I wanted to hug Krista in Rachel's place. Instead, I said, "Go back to bed. I'll see you in a couple of hours."

I was shivering by the time I reached Rachel at the doorway. "Do you think we'll all stay in touch?"

"Probably not," she said as she unlocked the door. "Krista's fine but I've had enough of Brenda."

"And of me?"

"Never. I'll call." She hugged me again.

I watched her get into her rental car and drive away. My suspicion drove away with her. She was a friend, not a murderer.

When I closed the door, I remembered to lock it.

* *

At dawn, I gave up trying to sleep and went downstairs to shower. I made sure the door was still locked, started the coffee, then went into the bathroom. The Calderwood crest image that had been painted on the cabinet was streaked with black paint. More of Brenda's destruction that I hadn't seen because I'd been using the upstairs bathroom. The angry black lines froze me, but the shower warmed my body. The silence of the house felt like a threat. When I dried myself, I thought about the towels. They were impossibly white because Brenda never had guests. The towels, the bedding, everything was for show, not for use.

I climbed the stairs to my bedroom, unable to shake off the idea that I was the uninvited guest, that Brenda had locked me out of the house on purpose. The door to her studio was still closed and Krista was still sleeping. I picked up my wet sneakers, determined to walk off my anxiety. I carried them downstairs and poured myself a cup of coffee in one of the half-dozen pottery mugs from New Hampshire's Salmon Falls Stoneware. Its familiar blueberry embossment was more comforting than a Calderwood crest mug would have been.

I went into the living room and set the mug on the coffee table while I put on my sneakers. My socks wouldn't stay dry for long, but the day promised to be warm enough to wear sandals later. I turned the key to unlock the door to the front porch. The back door had been latched from the inside. I tried not to suspect Brenda. If Nelson entered the house and latched it, he would have left through the porch. Or maybe it was Maureen. She knew the house well. She could easily have found her way in the fog.

I retrieved my coffee and went outside into the cool morning air. The fog had lifted and steam was rising from the wet grass into the clearing sky. Seagulls swooped the horizon. Holding my coffee cup so it warmed my hands, I descended the stairs. At the bottom, broken on the grass, I saw what I tripped on in the night.

A wine bottle. The label lay face up, identifying it as a chenin blanc from some vineyard named Royal. It wasn't a wine we brought and it wasn't one we'd been drinking from Gerald's collection. I needed to confront Brenda about it, but first I needed to walk.

Instead of heading toward the ocean and the beach where we'd seen the red-haired man, I walked toward the tiny town of Bristol. I stayed on the left side, facing any cars that might be coming into the Cove. The road was curvy with only a narrow shoulder. But it was so early and so quiet I felt like I could walk down the middle and not be in danger. Until a car sped by heading away from the Cove. The driver was in a hurry.

I came around a curve and saw someone in the distance walking a dog. As we approached each other, the dog began barking. "She's friendly," said the woman walking it even as the dog, some large variety of retriever, pulled on the leash toward me.

Instead of saying, "I'm not," I stepped away from it and said, "It's a beautiful morning."

I continued walking to a road that turned to the left. It brought me down a short hill to a restaurant that was closed. Anyone who wanted breakfast would have to go into Bristol. Condominiums lined the slope across from the restaurant. The older prestigious homes of Calderwood Cove had been infiltrated by the new.

A runner stopped in front of one of the condos and bent to catch his breath. He waved to a woman on the porch. Maybe his wife or a neighbor. A woman emerged from another condo with two children carrying tennis rackets. They got into an SUV and waved to me when the car passed.

The Cove was waking up. Brenda and Krista should be as well, so I began my walk back, this time on the side of the road where any cars would be coming away from the ocean and heading toward Bristol. Before I saw it, I heard the squeak of

Peter's Volkswagen. He slowed when he saw me then stopped, lowered his passenger side window, and leaned toward me. "You're out early."

"I couldn't sleep. You know what happened last night."

"Something happened?"

"I heard you talking to Nelson when the police released him."

A car came around the corner and slammed on its brakes.

"You know as much as I do. I'll see you later." He drove away so the car wouldn't have to pass him.

I dumped the last of my coffee onto the road. I needed a hot cup. Esther must have been watching from her window because as soon as I reached Brenda's house, she called me over to hers.

"Come inside." She was still in her bathrobe, its sleeves covered in flour. "I'll give you some scones."

The smell of baking pastry filled the house. Baking must have been her way of comforting herself. She left me standing in the living room where I could see Nelson at the dining room table. I was happy to stay away from him.

Esther returned with four giant blueberry scones. "I made these with the berries you gave me yesterday."

They were still warm and smelled delicious. "Want to take one of them back? Rachel left early this morning."

"No matter. You'll eat them. I hope you're staying longer."

"Just until tomorrow. Krista's leaving in a little while."

"It's good you've been here for Brenda." She glanced back at Nelson. "And for me."

I was glad that she followed me onto her porch. "What did Nelson say last night?"

"He doesn't know anything about an oyster fraud."

I doubted that but I was willing to let Esther keep her illusions. "Did you ask him about the envelopes?"

She wrapped her bathrobe more tightly. "You told the police

about the one he gave to that guy on a bike. I won't need to tell them about the other one. Nelson explained."

She stopped talking when a plane flew overhead. I wanted it to be Rachel's flight, but the plane was too small and Calderwood Cove wasn't in Portland's flight path. "Well?" I said when the noise died down.

"Damn summer people. Think they can fly over the Cove and take photos of their fancy houses."

"You must hate the changes you've seen."

"More to come, I'm afraid. Enjoy the scones." She started to go into the house.

"Wait. You didn't tell me what was in those envelopes."

"Just a bit of money for the man on the bike. Nelson won't give him a job but he gave him enough for a bit of food."

I suspected Nelson wasn't that generous. "And the one he gave to Gerald? Did you ask Nelson?"

"I will later. Eat those scones while they're warm."

She went into the house, leaving me to wonder what was really in those envelopes.

I crossed the street to Brenda's and I entered through the back door. She or Krista had unlocked it. I heard one of them in the shower. No one had taken any of the coffee I'd made. I put one of the scones on my plate, refilled my coffee mug, and went onto the porch to wait.

It didn't take long before Krista joined me with her own scone and some coffee. "Compliments of Esther? Are these as good as they look?"

"They are." As soon as she sat down, I told her about the locked door and the wine bottle.

"Maybe Brenda got up for more wine and locked the door. I didn't hear anything until I saw you and Rachel."

"That broken wine bottle's a chenin blanc. Were you drinking that with your pie when I was at Esther's?"

"We weren't drinking anything except coffee and tea. Even Brenda. After you went back to Esther's, she and Rachel had a yelling match. Rachel said Brenda was better off without Gerald. She'd have freedom and money of her own. Brenda said Rachel was cruel. She loved her husband. Rachel accused her of lying. That's when I said we all needed to go to bed. I barely kept her from accusing Brenda of murder."

I heard the squeak of Peter's car across the street. Wherever he was going when he passed me, he hadn't gone far.

Brenda opened the door. "Peter should fix that damn squeak. It drove me nuts yesterday." She sat between Krista and me. Her hands were shaking so much she had trouble keeping her scone and her coffee from crashing onto the porch floor.

"Are you ready to tell us why you brought him to a lawyer?" Krista shaded her eyes from the morning sun.

Brenda sipped coffee before she answered. She had to hold the cup with both hands. "Deborah knows. Peter and I have been talking about turning the cottage into an artists' retreat. Leo Foster is helping with some paperwork."

"That's awfully sudden." Krista sounded shocked.

"We've been planning it for a while. Now things have changed."

Krista stood up. She barely controlled her voice when she said, "Couldn't you at least wait until you buried your husband?"

"Easy for you to say. Gerald's finances were complicated. Leo and Peter will both help me sort through them."

I wanted Krista to leave without getting into an argument with Brenda. I changed the subject. "Never mind. Tell me about last night. Did you get up and lock the back door? I had to find my way in the fog to the front."

"Weren't you inside?" Brenda's smile told me she knew I wasn't.

"No. I tripped over that wine bottle that's broken at the bottom of the stairs. Did you come outside and drink a whole bottle by yourself?"

"I'm not that much of a lush. Peter came over with that bottle. We talked about our plans. I locked the door when he left."

I'd heard Peter and Nelson at midnight. He and Brenda knew I was still waiting with Esther. He had to have known about the police. And Brenda locked me out on purpose.

Krista started toward the door. "I'm ready to pack up and go home."

"I thought you were going to stay until noon." I wanted her company.

"Pack and you can follow Deborah and me to the cemetery. See what it means to be a Calderwood. You can drive home from there." Brenda was ready for Krista to leave. I wondered what that meant for me.

CHAPTER 17

B RENDA DROVE HER BMW through an arched gateway with the name Island Cemetery carved across the top. Krista followed in her yellow mini-wagon while I felt like I was riding with Brenda in a hearse. All around us, trees, leafy or pine-needled, dotted grass that was kept green in the ocean air. We parked in front of what looked like the largest headstone and got out of the cars. I read the name Calderwood on what was more a monument than a headstone. It was the tallest in the cemetery, a marble obelisk amid simple granite markers. An etching of the family crest filled the place on the stone where older stones would have a death's-head or an hourglass or a weeping willow. The Calderwood stone showed two names. Gerald Mackinnon Calderwood, April 28, 1968 – and Brenda Calderwood, November 2, 1973 –. She wasn't identified as Brenda Peterson Calderwood. The omitted middle name made her feel like Gerald's possession.

Smaller Calderwood headstones surrounded the one Gerald had obviously commissioned. Wherever they'd lived during the winter, they'd chosen to be buried in Calderwood Cove. Tobias and Nellie. Benjamin and Cordelia. Wellington and Elizabeth. The man's name always came ahead of the woman's no matter who had died first. Some of the stones had the names of children carved beneath the parents' names. I could see that these were children who died young. They hadn't married and been given a plot of their own.

The earliest dates I saw were for Barclay and Aisla Calderwood, both born in 1797. The founders of the Calderwood clan, I assumed. Not as old as I'd thought. Some of the gravestones in Shelby dated to the 1600s. None of these headstones had epitaphs or the iconography that were reminders of death. A few had carved scrolls, but most were plain with only the names of the deceased.

I looked again at the ostentatious monument to Gerald. His stone was the only one with an epitaph. "He honored the name to the end."

I pointed to it. "What does the epitaph mean?"

Brenda laughed. "Gerald thought he was the last direct descendent of Barclay and Aisla."

"That's an odd thing to be proud of," said Krista, who was standing directly in front of the headstone, her hands clasped behind her back.

Brenda laughed again, as if in triumph, "It wasn't even true. There is my son."

"Your son will never know it." I remembered what Brenda had said about being free and alone.

Brenda kicked the headstone. "But I will."

Krista drew her away. "I don't understand. If Gerald was proud enough of being a Calderwood to have this headstone carved before he died, why isn't there going to be a casket and a burial? You had him cremated."

For the third time, Brenda laughed. "Yesterday Leo Foster told me about Gerald's instructions for a coffin. Expensive and ornate. It was too late. We'll shovel his ashes into a pit in front of this ridiculous headstone. He could control me in life, but he can't control me in death. Let's get out of here."

I stepped away from the Calderwood plot to the one next to it and the stone that said "Timothy Clayton Sproul 1929 – 1956 and Esther Bristol Sproul 1930 –" and "Nelson Bristol Sproul 1953 –" under it.

I read the history in the simple engravings. Esther had been well-connected, a Bristol for whom the town was named. Her husband died when he was only twenty-seven and she'd raised Nelson alone. A geranium had been planted in front of the stone.

As we left the Calderwood graves to get into our cars, I read the surname on one more family plot. Foster. The name of Brenda's lawyer. Embedded on the ground was a simple slab and the name Udevilla Foster. 1838 – 1935. With the 'a' ending, I assumed Udevilla had been a woman, likely a spinster because hers was the only name on the stone. A geranium like the one in the Sproul plot flowered in front of it. Whoever she'd been, she'd lived to be almost a hundred. Someone, maybe Esther, still remembered her. Gerald's preparations for his own remembrance wouldn't include someone to plant flowers in front of his name.

When we reached our cars, Brenda looked back at the cemetery and asked, "Do you ever visit Joseph Wheeler's grave?"

"When his mother died, Rachel and I left roses. It was winter so it was only a gesture. I don't plant flowers but I often walk in the cemetery. There's a grave there for a child who died at age three in 1840."

"Because she reminds you of your daughter?" asked Krista as she opened her car door.

"Yes. It helps me remember." I resisted telling them that I talked every night to Cathy and Nathan's ashes that were mingled in an urn next to my bed.

Krista hugged me. "I'll visit. We can walk through the cemetery together. We'll plant flowers for Joseph and his mother and that little girl."

"There'll be no cemetery for me. I'll never be buried in that plot Gerald planned." Brenda hugged Krista in a way she hadn't hugged Rachel at dawn. "Thank you for coming." As we watched Krista drive away, she said, "Car's just like Krista. Sunshine yellow. She still annoys me."

"She was a help this weekend."

"Whatever." Brenda got into her hearse-like car and started the engine before I'd gotten into the passenger side.

I looked out the side window along the tree-lined road that would take us back to Calderwood Cove. The landscape was lush and alive. After a few miles, I broke the dead silence of the car. "Do you want to talk about it?"

She kept her eyes on the road. "About what?"

"About Gerald. About what you'll do now."

"I have my plans."

"The artists' retreat? Want to share more about it?" In answer, she turned on the car radio.

When we arrived at her house, she parked and went immediately to her mailbox as if she was expected something. She pulled out a fistful of mail and thumbed through it. When we got inside, she threw it on the dining room table. "Will you take something over to Peter? I need to stay here and paint over that awful crest on my mailbox."

She disappeared upstairs. I resisted an urge to look through her mail. It wasn't long before I convinced myself that I should look for anything that might be a clue to Gerald's murder. There wasn't much, a sale flyer for Renys, an envelope from Maine's Republican Party, a letter addressed to Gerald with a return address from a Boston architectural firm that made me wonder if he was considering renovations to their Boston apartment and what Brenda would do with it now that he was dead. The only piece of mail for her was from River Arts in Damariscotta. If this was what she was waiting for, maybe she also decided before Gerald's death to sell her paintings.

I straightened the mail when I heard her on the stairs. She appeared, carrying a canvas the size of a legal pad and the art supply box I'd seen near her easel. She handed me the canvas. It was a painting of Esther's house. A few clouds above the house mimicked a passing storm, a rainbow arcing out of them and disappearing behind the roof line. Above the section of what was now Peter's apartment, I could just read a sign that said Bristol Ship Building.

"This is lovely." I ran my hand over smooth brush strokes that showed none of the agitation in the painting of us she'd hung on her studio door. "Is it for Peter?"

"What would he want with a painting like this. It's for Esther. Peter and I bought a frame when we were in Damariscotta. He's going to frame it and we'll give it to her. Her birthday's July fourteenth."

I remembered the gravestone that carved 1930 next to Esther's name. "Her ninety-second?"

"Something like that. The rainbow's a cliché, but Esther will like it."

I followed her outside and left her opening her paints at the mailbox. Esther might be outside in her garden, so I held the painting against my chest. The garden was empty, saving me from having to think up a lie about what I was doing. Peter answered the door to his apartment as I knocked.

He took the painting from me and studied it a moment. "A bit of a cliché but Esther will love it."

"That's exactly what Brenda said."

"Come inside. I'll show you the frame." He spoke in the cadence I'd noticed before in his voice. I wanted him to show me some of his poems as well.

The interior of what had once been a space for building ships astonished me. A walled-off section adjacent to the main house must be the bathroom. Along that side, a kitchen area opened into the rest of the room. It was too wide for a ship's galley, but it was built to replicate one with its hanging cast-iron pots and pans. An empty take-out box sat open on the wooden counter next to a plate of blueberry scones. Esther took good care of Peter.

The wall space opposite the kitchen was filled with built-in shelves and drawers. Under the only window at the front of the room, a bench looked like it opened into a bed. The window was huge, fashioned from what had once been a door large enough to move ships in and out. The ceiling's rounded contour was fashioned like the interior of a wooden dome. All the wood in the room was stained a light pine color and polished to a high sheen.

Under a chandelier of lights made to look like ship lanterns, a table was littered with papers and a laptop computer. Only a long extension cord that kept the laptop plugged in spoiled the feeling of being in a luxury stateroom at the turn into the twentieth century. Even the sofa and matching chair were upholstered in a dark blue velvet that might have been popular then. A scattering of Persian area rugs pulled the room together and kept it from feeling cavernous.

"Wow," I said as I gave Peter the canvas.

"Nelson thought of every detail."

"Or Esther."

"Whoever. Look at this. He reached into an opening on a miniature navigational quadrant to switch on an overhead light. "Nothing to break the ship's atmosphere. Come see the frame."

I followed him to the table. Unlike the highly polished room, the rectangular plank was gouged with marks that looked like they'd been made by forks and knives. It was a smaller version of the one in Brenda's dining room.

Peter rested the painting on top of a plain gray frame that captured the gray of the few storm clouds that seemed to spit out the rainbow.

"Good choice," I said. "The frame matches the storm clouds."

"She's had more storms in her life than she deserves. Right now she's worried that she'll have to sell this house. Live in Damariscotta even in the summer."

I ran my fingers along the rough lines of the table. "She's worried about the oyster farm. I heard you talking with Nelson about vibriosis in Gerald's body. Is he running into trouble with contaminated oysters?"

"He's worried about global warming. Everyone's running into trouble with oyster farming. The ocean's warming too much. Great for tourism, though."

"You said she's had storms. Did something bad happen to her? She seems pretty resilient to me."

"Her husband died when Nelson was three years old. Esther raised him herself."

"At least she had a child to raise." If my Cathy survived the car crash, I would have been overjoyed to raise her on my own. I decided not to tell Peter my story. I didn't want it turned into a poem. "How did her husband die?"

"Crushed right about where you're standing. A ship he was working on fell away from one of the ropes that was holding it up."

I looked at the ceiling and imagined a ship instead of a chandelier hanging down. "How awful. You must be spending a lot of time with Esther to have learned her story."

"Sometimes I play cribbage with her. She's a bit like Brenda. Not too sad about her husband's death. Problem was the shipbuilding business belonged to the Bristols. He was supposed to manage it. After he died, she found out it was sunk in debt. She sold the business, but not this place. About ten years ago, Nelson decided to turn it into a rental property."

"Or Esther did." For the second time, I gave her credit that Peter wanted to give to Nelson.

"Doesn't matter who. If that oyster farm goes under, there'll be no income."

"The apartment would bring in money. She could charge a lot for it."

"I know. I'm lucky to get it in exchange for doing a few odd jobs and keeping an old lady company."

"Does it inspire you to write?"

"Not so much." He paused and looked out the window before answering. "I write about outside things."

"Can I see some of your work?"

"Maybe tomorrow. I have an appointment in Damariscotta."

"Do you go there often? I saw you go out the night of the fireworks. Much later I heard someone talking. It sounded like that man who keeps riding around on his bicycle."

"I hate fireworks. I escaped them and went to a bar in Damariscotta. When I came back, I saw that guy hanging around the cottage. I told him to get out."

"Did you tell the police?"

"Nothing really to tell. But I will if you want me to."

"Yes, I think you should. I'm leaving tomorrow, but I'll stop by to say goodbye, maybe see a couple of your poems."

"Please do," he said and showed me to the door.

As I crossed the street, I could see that Brenda had finished painting the mailbox. The Calderwood crest was still visible beneath a covering of red x's. The x's were loud. They looked more like a threat than a declaration of a family name.

CHAPTER 18

AFTER MY TALK with Peter about Esther, I retreated to Brenda's porch, thinking about why the G-man was in Brenda's cottage and wondering if he tripped the light sensor that I noticed the night we learned of Gerald's murder. I was stretched on the lounge reading *Moby-Dick*. I wasn't like Ishmael who went to sea whenever he felt a damp November in his soul, but I chose it so I would be reminded of the call of the ocean. I'd reached Chapter forty-two on the Whiteness of the Whale and had begun to feel like Ahab chasing the human white whale who had capsized Gerald's boat against the rocks at Pemiquid Light. Last night's fog had engulfed me in Moby Dick's shroud-like whiteness.

With Rachel and Krista both gone, Brenda frightened me. Her laughter at the cemetery was like a madwoman's. In between pages, I watched her at the porch railing where she'd been staring at the horizon for the last hour. Voices at the side of the house startled both of us. Holland and Abu appeared.

Holland called to us. "Here you are. We knocked at the back door. Can we come up?"

They didn't wait for an answer. I jumped off the lounge and stood next to them where they'd planted themselves in front of Brenda. She slowly turned from the railing, barely acknowledging them.

Holland wasted no time telling us why they were here. "We found Gerald's boat."

"Oh." Brenda's word sounded like an alto "om," neither a comment nor a question.

I asked what she should have. "Where was it? Did you find anything in it to explain Gerald's death?"

"Forensics is going over it now. Some kids—"

Holland interrupted Abu. "Kids found it on the rocks at Inner Heron Island. We've got someone looking at the tide, but we figure whoever killed Gerald dumped his body first then got off the boat somewhere near the tip of Calderwood Cove, turned on the motor, and pointed the boat out to sea. It didn't make it into the wider ocean."

"That's enough, Scotty." As he'd been doing, Abu stopped him from revealing more.

Holland's connection to people in the Cove continued to trump his role as sheriff. "Yuh, I know, Bashiir," he said. "I'll just ask Brenda one question." He looked at Brenda, who was leaning against the railing as if it could hold her up. "We know Gerald kept his boat at Calderwood Marina. Did he sometimes sail early with a friend?"

Brenda turned to look over the railing then turned back again, her brown eyes flashing anger. "Gerald never went sailing early. He was supposed to be on a flight to Hilton Head. Obviously, he's been lying to me."

"We'll come back after forensics goes over the boat. It's still pretty intact." Holland tried to be reassuring.

Brenda snapped at him. "It doesn't matter. I never liked that boat. Nothing more boring than sailing. Gerald only used the motor if he had to get back for some meeting."

Abu jumped on her comment. "What kind of meeting?"

Brenda laughed in the way she'd been laughing at the cemetery.

"How should I know. Gerald left his accounting firm two years ago."

Abu pressed further. "Do you know how he made his money after he left?"

"There must be a connection to Nelson and the oyster fraud," I blurted out, then covered myself by adding something they might not know. "Esther saw Nelson and Gerald arguing a week ago. Nelson gave Gerald an envelope and Gerald tore it up."

Abu and Holland looked at each other, their expressions confirming this was new information. "We'll follow up," said Abu.

"What about the red-haired man I told you about? I'm sure everything's connected."

"We talked with him. Gerry—"

Abu stopped Holland before he said more, then spoke to me. "We're done for now. Let us do the investigating." He started toward the porch stairs. "We'll let you know if forensics finds anything Brenda should know about." He didn't share the information about vibriosis.

As soon as they disappeared, Brenda said, "I'm going upstairs to paint."

I tossed aside my book. Ahab's monomania could wait. I had my own need to pursue a killer before I left Calderwood Cove.

I went down the porch stairs and headed toward the little beach, the rhythm of my steps accompanying the rhythm of my thoughts. I didn't feel threatened. It was a warm summer afternoon during Fourth of July week. The beach wouldn't be crowded but there should be people there, at least some of those kids who'd passed Esther's singing "American Pie."

Voices rose from the Beach Club. A tennis match was in progress and a group sat in lawn chairs at the edge of the court. I could hear grunts as loud as Maria Sharapova's and Rafael

Nadal's. The beach could wait. I turned down the hill to the Club where rumors about the oyster fraud would be spreading as fast as a tennis serve.

A woman got up from a canvas chair that had Calderwood Beach Club painted on the back. "Are you a new member?" she said.

I recognized her voice as the one with the New Jersey accent I'd heard when we were picking blueberries. The woman who'd been attracted to Gerald's blue eyes. "No membership. I'm staying with Brenda Calderwood."

"She's required to accompany any guests." New Jersey sounded like the designated bouncer.

"I didn't know. I just thought I might be able to get a drink of water."

She pointed to a glass jug filled with water, ice, and lemon. "Help yourself."

I picked up a glass next to the water dispenser. The grunts from one of the men on the court were loud enough they could have shattered my glass. It was etched with the Calderwood crest. I used that to open a conversation. "Gerald Calderwood must have donated these. I recognize the crest."

"He was a wonderful man. Warm and generous." She praised Gerald in a way no one else had.

"Did you know him well?"

She blushed. "Well enough. Are the police making any progress finding his murderer?"

I pretended innocence. "Has his death been officially called a murder?"

"One of our members is Scotty Holland's cousin. With Scotty and that Somali guy investigating, I'm afraid they'll never find out what happened."

"I guess you don't think much of the Maine police."

"I've nothing against them. They never get criminal cases to build their skills. Maine's too placid." Another grunt and an outburst of curses from the court didn't sound placid.

I seized the opening. "There's also a case involving an oyster fraud. Do you know anything about that?"

"Nelson Sproul's a member. He has nothing to do with it. Maybe that mother of his. She's old but she's devious."

"I guess you heard about last night."

"The Cove's a small place. Word travels fast." She turned to the court to shut off any more conversation.

I set my glass in a plastic tub alongside other dirty glasses. Most had limes in them, evidence that the few people watching the match preferred gin and tonic to water. I watched a serve. A man in white tennis shorts tossed the ball and reached high to slam it into a perfect position shy of the back line. His opponent was small but quick. He returned the serve so it landed just over the net. White shorts lunged for it, missed, and threw down his racket. "You killed me. Next game'll be mine."

He picked up his racket and came off the court toward the woman I'd been talking with. He stopped where I stood in front of the water jug. "Who are you?" He scanned my body, his face wet with sweat.

"A friend of Brenda Calderwood. I stopped to ask for water. I'm leaving now."

He took a towel from the New Jersey woman and wiped his face. "Not so fast. If you're with Brenda, maybe you know more about why the police came here on the Fourth. Got our membership roll from my wife." He nodded toward New Jersey, his own accent as strong as hers. "They interviewed all of us as if we knew something about Gerald's plans for the weekend."

"Did you?" Behind him I could see two couples walk onto the court for a mixed doubles match.

"Only that he wouldn't be here for our Fourth of July party. He usually gave a toast before the fireworks started. Always snuck in something about the Cove and the original Calderwoods. A little too proud of his ancestry in my book but my wife liked him." He tried to hand a sweat-soaked towel to her, but she refused to take it. I could feel the negative energy between them. She moved back to the chair she'd been in when I arrived.

"Do you serve raw oysters at your club?"

"Doing a little investigating yourself, are you?" He spoke as if he knew about the vibriosis. Holland might try to be professional in front of Abu, but he seemed to keep his cousin informed. Like the New Jersey woman said, the Cove was a small place.

The tennis match had started, two on a side, couple battling couple. "Did Gerald play tennis?" I wanted to move our conversation about oysters to Gerald's tennis or golf and Hilton Head.

"Strictly a golf man. A bit slow for my taste. Bad as those folks." He indicated the mixed doubles' match. The players were moving at half the speed he and his opponent had kept.

"Did Gerald say anything about going to Hilton Head for a golf tournament?"

"Jesus. He should have returned that serve."

I waited while he watched the tennis players before I asked again. "Did you know about the golf tournament? Brenda invited me and some other friends almost a year ago when she knew he'd be away. He must have bragged about it."

"Gerald was pompous about his ancestry, but he didn't share anything personal. Besides, we were gone all winter. He mentioned it to me on Memorial Day. A few weeks later, he said he wouldn't be here on the Fourth and I asked if it was because of the tournament in Hilton Head. All he said was that he was going there for a meeting, not a tournament, and the meeting place had changed."

"Did he say what meeting? Where it was changed to?"

"What's making you so free with all the questions?"

"Brenda's my friend. I'd like to find out who killed her husband."

"I can't help you. All Gerald said was that it involved some kind of financial opportunity." He threw the towel he was still holding over his shoulder and started toward the clubhouse.

I walked away from the Beach Club and up the hill to the road. I hadn't learned much. The New Jersey woman liked Gerald and disliked both Brenda and Esther. She might even have been having an affair with Gerald. She seemed to prefer him to the husband she rebuffed when she refused to take his towel. He'd revealed something the police might be following up on. Gerald wasn't going to Hilton Head only to play golf. There'd been a meeting scheduled and that meeting was changed. Who else had canceled reservations in Hilton Head?

I stopped at the road to call Abu with the information. He answered quickly. "Deborah. Have you learned something else?"

"Gerald was going to Hilton Head for a meeting about some kind of financial opportunity." I wanted to say it might involve real estate, to tell him about Gerald's property in Shelby, but I kept my information general. I didn't want to say that Rachel had Gerald's name in her contact list. "Did anyone else cancel reservations? Was anyone from around here going to be in Hilton Head?"

"You'd make a good detective. Palmetto Dunes could give us no further information. Call again if you learn something helpful."

I heard his tone of dismissal. He was right. I should let the police do their work.

I started walking again and caught up with a group of four teenagers who were carrying towels and tossing a bright blue frisbee back and forth.

"You're wrong," the tallest boy said as he threw the frisbee at a girl with a thick braid that swung as she caught it.

"What makes you so sure?" She stooped to pick up the frisbee she missed.

"Lonnie and I saw him at his boat last week. He was loading it up. Told us he was spending the Fourth on the ocean."

The other boy, who must have been Lonnie, said, "I asked him if he was going alone. He said he was going with a friend."

"Well it wasn't his wife. She's a bitch." The girl in the group whose hair was as short as the braided girl's was long put her hands up to catch the frisbee. When she saw me behind them, she held onto it. "Enough frisbee for now. We're at the beach."

I slowed so they could get ahead of me. Were they right? Was Gerald planning a trip with a woman or were they being teenage gossips?

When I reached the little cove the locals called a beach, they'd dropped their towels on the rocks and were splashing in the water, daring each other to swim in the cold Atlantic. The man with the red hair—Gerry—was reclining at the back of the beach watching them, his legs thrust out in front of him. I could smell the marijuana he was smoking. He saw me and held out his joint. "Want a toke?"

I didn't, but if I said yes maybe he'd say something over a shared joint that he wouldn't tell the police. When I sat next to him, the rocks dug into me. "Puff, puff, pass," he said as he handed the joint to me. The first hit surprised me. This wasn't the mild marijuana of my college years.

"You're not much of a smoker," he said.

"It's been a while. Gerald Calderwood's house isn't exactly a place to start again."

"He was more uptight than Nelson Sproul."

My head was already buzzing. "So you know—knew—them

both. Esther told me you were asking Nelson for a job."

"Who's Esther?"

I copied his marijuana etiquette, took another puff, and said, "Pass. Esther is Nelson's mother."

"The old lady. What kind of guy would still be livin' with his mother?" He toked in deeply, his red hair framing a face so gaunt he looked like he needed a mother to feed him.

"Is Maureen your mother? Leroy your father? You have his red hair."

He puffed and passed, speaking slowly. "Coincidence. I was adopted. I left that house as soon as I turned eighteen."

I passed a last time. I'd had more puffing than I could handle. He inhaled deeply then blew out a smoke ring that floated above his eyes that were as blue as Joseph Wheeler's eyes when Rachel and I found him on the floor of the barn. As blue as Gerald Calderwood's. As blue as the frisbee that lay on the beach. My brain was spinning marijuana metaphors. "Your name's Gerry. Was Gerald Calderwood your biological father? Is that why you're here?"

"Don't know. Don't care. Maureen and Leroy move around a lot. One of the problems when I was a kid. I could never settle into any school or group of friends. Look at those kids swimmin'. They've probably been friends since elementary school."

All except the girl with the long braid had managed to get into the water. The short-haired girl and the tall boy were swimming away from the shore into the frigid bay. The other boy came out of the water and found his towel. I saw him shivering.

"They're summer friends. They probably lead entirely separate lives in the winter."

"Rich kids have fancy phones. They stay in contact." I could hear the loneliness in his voice turning to anger.

"Where did you grow up?" I couldn't identify his accent, only his dropped *g*s.

"I told you. We moved around a lot."

"What about now? How did you find Maureen and Leroy?"

"They found me in Boston. They want to put me in drug rehab. Don't know how they suddenly have that much money."

Still holding the joint, he managed to get onto his feet.

I stood up next to him, able to see how emaciated his body was. Whatever else the O'Donnells were, they knew that he needed help. "Did Nelson give you a job?" I said, suspecting he was involved with more drugs than marijuana.

"Nope."

"What was in the envelope he gave you?"

He puffed before he answered. "Money."

"For what?"

He took his second puff and tried to hand the joint to me. "To keep me quiet."

I refused the puff. "Was that why you wanted $5,000 from Gerald?"

He toked again. He wasn't going to waste the last of the joint. "What makes you say that?"

"I told you at Renys. I recognized your voice when you called looking for Gerald."

He nearly burned his fingers on the end of the joint. He buried it in the sand before he answered. "I told him I knew something was going on between him and Maureen and Leroy."

"Do you know what?"

"Nope again. But somethin' was and it's worth money. There's a reason Maureen and Leroy left. They never get too close to whatever scheme they're involved in."

"What kind of schemes?"

"Always changes. Probably somethin' about oysters this time."

"Will you look for your parents? Let them help you?"

"Whatever," he said through a mellow haze then added, "I never call them my parents." His mellow haze had turned nasty. I was relieved when he left me on the beach alone with the teenagers who were now all out of the water and throwing the frisbee back and forth.

I waited a few minutes. Gerry told me only a little more than I already knew. He was adopted, Maureen and Leroy moved around a lot and were likely involved in the oyster fraud. What I didn't know was how this connected to Gerald's murder. Or why this drug-addled, adopted son was named Gerry.

I walked alongside the teenagers and caught the frisbee that was flying toward the girl with the braid. I sailed it back to the girl with the short hair, who sent it back to me. I flew it one more time, called out thanks and left the beach, my steps slower than usual. The marijuana buzz I still felt amplified my thoughts of tainted oysters and red-haired, blue-eyed men and murder.

CHAPTER 19

T HE GRANDFATHER CLOCK was striking four when I came into the house through the back door. The last chime of the clock echoed like Rachel's warning that Brenda might have killed Gerald. I went into the kitchen for a glass of water. As I drank, I stared at the knife block on the counter. It was still missing the knife Brenda had used to destroy Gerald's clothing and the Calderwood crest sign, but now another knife was also gone. I rinsed my glass, hoping to see it in the sink. The sink was empty and the dish rack held only the plates we'd used for Esther's scones. I had to stop imagining Brenda as a murderer. And Nelson and Maureen and Leroy and G-man Gerry. Even Rachel.

I needed to leave, to follow Krista into the safe haven of our homes, to let Brenda play the grieving widow tomorrow. I couldn't share Rachel's suggestion that she killed her husband. Brenda could be difficult but she wasn't a killer. The police didn't suspect her. All their questions had been about Gerald and how she might remember something that would lead them to his killer.

Still, I wanted to leave. I glanced at the empty knife slot and started upstairs to pack my suitcase. I stopped in front of Brenda's studio where I saw her cleaning paintbrushes.

"You're here." She picked up the missing kitchen knife and began wiping it.

I stepped backward.

She looked at her hands. Her tremor was controlled. "It's just a paring knife. I got the most amazing lines using it. Come see."

In the middle of a canvas that she'd painted a smooth black, she'd created a wild splash of turquoise with paint so thick it would take days to dry. Within the uncontrolled splash, she'd used the knife point to etch a tree. The knife marks revealed a black coating underneath the turquoise. The effect created the fine lines of a pencil drawing, wavy but precise. They contrasted with the violence of the turquoise background. It was frightening.

She finished wiping the knife and set it down. "What do you think?"

I took a minute to compose an answer. "It's an interesting technique. I always admire artists who have the patience to draw those tiny lines."

"I didn't draw them. I cut them. Like a surgeon."

Or a murderer, I thought, before I said, "I came upstairs to pack. I should go home tonight, not wait until morning. I have a lot of work to do."

"Please don't. The house is too quiet. I'm not used to being alone." Her hands started to tremble. She was like someone with ADHD instead of bipolar disorder. Whatever control she'd mustered for her knife etching was gone.

"You'll be okay." I started out of the room.

She followed me. "Wait. Just one more night. A sleepover like when we were kids. We'll walk to Bayside. I'll tell you something I found out at the lawyer's."

I understood what she meant about being alone. The first nights after Nathan and Cathy died, they inhabited the house. When I dozed, Nathan reached for me in the bed. Cathy cried from her room. When I woke, the house was silent. It went on night after night until I managed to give away their things and claim the house for myself while I decided what to do next. Coming back to Shelby and going to Simmons for a degree in library science had helped me to heal. Brenda, Rachel, Krista, me. We'd been friends since we were six years old. Whether Benda was begging me or bribing me, I could manage one more night.

"I'll leave in the morning," I said.

Her thank you was genuine. "It's early, but let's go to Bayside. I never ate lunch."

My empty stomach told me I hadn't eaten since my morning scone. I'd only taken three hits, but the marijuana had made me starving. "We'll call it the Early Bird Special. Just wait until I change."

"You're fine."

I wasn't fine. My pants were sandy from sitting on the beach and I could smell the marijuana on my T-shirt. I looked more disheveled than sporty. "Just give me a second." I went into my room and found my jeans and the long-sleeved T-shirt with the Town of Shelby logo I'd worn the morning after we arrived.

Brenda was waiting for me at the top of the stairs. She'd taken off her painting smock and was wearing a silk shirt over her designer jeans. I envied how she managed to look glamorous even for an Early Bird Special. We descended the stairs together and left the house, unlocked.

As soon as we started down the road I'd walked in the morning, Peter's Volkswagen appeared around a corner. He pulled to the side and stopped. When we reached him, he leaned toward his rolled down window and spoke only to Brenda. "I did what you asked. I had to hunt a bit for ones still blooming. The florist said she could manage. She was surprised. The minister had already ordered roses and lilies. I told her he should have talked to you first."

"Thanks. I'll see you later. Deborah and I are going for an Early Bird Special."

"Life begins at widowhood." Peter shifted into gear and drove away.

"What was that all about?" I asked as we turned onto the road that led to Bayside.

"I wasn't lying when I told you Peter and I made funeral arrangements before we saw a lawyer. I told Reverend Jackson to do all the planning. Gerald dragged me to church just often enough that he knew my husband. Upstanding community member and all that."

"So the minister ordered flowers as well as planned the service?"

"Apparently. After Peter and I left the lawyer, I saw a field of lupine. Gerald hated lupine, called them invasive weeds. I asked Peter to pick some and take them to the florist. It's my quiet revenge. That and the hymn I told Reverend Jackson to include. 'How Great Thou Art.' Gerald hated that even more than lupine. Said God wasn't great, only men were."

"Calderwood men?"

"You could say that."

We reached the house where I'd seen the family leave for tennis lessons. The children were running up and down the slope that served as a front yard. Tennis or croquet was impossible for these condos that were constructed on a hill.

Brenda pointed to them. "Imagine a dozen of these on the lawn in front of my house." She emphasized "my."

"Were there old homes here before the condos were built?"

"Just one. It belonged to the Sproul family. Nelson's father sold it when he was planning to open his oyster farm. It was a new and prosperous opportunity in Maine. Better than the timber industry he was involved in and that was floundering with a budworm infestation on the spruce trees. The new owner lived in it for a few summers then tore it down and built these.

Monstrosities, Nelson calls them. The same thing won't happen to my house now."

A young woman opened the wooden door to Bayside and unlatched the screen. We'd be the first ones to the Early Bird Special. "You said 'now.' Why would it happen to your house?"

"Let's wait until we're seated. We'll sit on the deck, Marina." Brenda nodded to the woman, who wore a sleeveless dress. The necklace that fell just above a hint of cleavage was made of polished beach stones.

"I'm sorry about Gerald," said Marina as she picked up two menus from the reception podium. "He was a nice man. Always generous with his tips."

Brenda murmured a thank you. "A bottle of chardonnay. Our usual one from California," she said in a way that told me she and Gerald often ate at Bayside. The waitress knew their wine and was another woman who liked Gerald. Maybe he wasn't as bad as Brenda and Esther made him out to be.

Marina placed the menus on a table set for four in the corner of the deck. Brenda and I sat down, kitty-corner to each other so we both had a view of the bay and the boats on the marina.

"The waitress's name," I said. "Was she named for the marina?"

"I suppose. Her father's the one who bought and developed the Sproul property. She lives in one of the condos. With her boyfriend, I think."

"What were you going to tell me about your house?"

A breeze was coming off the water and blowing hair into her face. It was a long as Rachel's but blond and when she pushed it back, she didn't play with it. "I found out at the lawyer's yesterday. Gerald was planning to sell the house to the same developer who built those condos."

Marina returned with the bottle of wine from a vineyard named Stony Hill. The label was simple and elegant, bare branches framing a bunch of grapes. While she poured some into our glasses, Brenda asked, "Did you know about it?"

Marina put the bottle into an ice bucket in the middle of the table. "About what?"

"Never mind. Come back in fifteen minutes and we'll order." When she was gone, Brenda picked up her wine glass. "Condos won't happen. The house is mine now. I'll get my artists' retreat." This time it was my hand that trembled as I filled my glass to meet her toast.

Brenda and I sat on her porch digesting our Early Bird Special. I wanted to go to bed, sleep through the night, get up and say goodbye to Calderwood Cove forever. But when you eat early in the summer, there's a long wait until sunset. We'd run out of things to say. Brenda was pretending to read the copy of *Wuthering Heights* she'd taken from the table in her sitting room.

I watched a chipmunk run across the grass and find a hole by one of the rocks in the garden. Would Gerald have pulled up that garden to squeeze in another condo unit? I couldn't understand why he would sell a place that held the Calderwood name he was so proud of.

Brenda slammed her book on the table. "I've had enough of this foggy novel."

"We need to do something. Walk off our dinner." I wanted to keep her from opening a bottle of wine.

"We already walked."

I looked out on the lawn where croquet had been set up the day we all arrived. "Let's play croquet. I remember how good you were at it."

"I still am. It beats the hell out of golf."

We climbed down from the porch and found the croquet set

tucked under the porch with the garden tools. I wished we had played when Rachel and Krista were still here. Any chance of that had been interrupted by Gerald's murder.

Brenda took a mallet and four wickets to one end of the lawn and I started at the other. After the rain and the fog of the seacoast, the post went into the grass easily. I positioned two wickets in front of the post then mirrored where Brenda was setting up the side wickets. We met in the middle, neither of us holding the last wicket we needed. When we said "I'll get it" at the same time, we laughed. A good game of croquet would help clear the air between us.

While I waited for her to get the last wicket, I realized I was standing where Nelson confronted Gerald with the envelope Gerald destroyed. I needed to find out about it before I left. Give Holland and Abu a final clue to Gerald's murder.

Brenda came back with the wicket and the ball she'd chosen. Orange. Last color on the post. No matter what color I chose, I'd have to go first. She'd have the advantage of having my ball ahead of hers to hit. She was competitive, always taking any advantages. Maybe even in her marriage to a man who offered money, if not love.

I chose the yellow ball and hit it through the wickets in front of the starting stake. I aimed my next shot at the wicket to the right side of our improvised court. The grass was thick and lush, not like the malnourished grass we'd played on as kids. My ball stopped well short of the wicket, but with the second shot I'd earned at the start, I set it up perfectly.

Brenda followed me. When her orange ball hit my yellow one out of position, she gloated. "I've been practicing."

"With Gerald?"

"God, no. He just liked to set croquet up on the lawn. Said it gives the place atmosphere. He was all about show."

When Nelson confronted him with an envelope, Gerald must have been setting up for a display, not a game. "I don't understand. If Gerald loved to announce the history of the house, why did he want to sell?"

Brenda sent her ball to the middle wicket.

"That's what Leo asked me."

"The lawyer?"

"Yes. He didn't know, but I think I do." She left me to try to center my ball so I could make it through the wicket on my next turn. I was going to lose badly. I caught up only after she missed an easy shot toward the second post at the end of the court. I went through the wickets first and hit the post. Before I took my shot back toward where we began, I said, "Do I get an answer?"

"An answer for what?"

"Why Gerald would sell this property that he likes to show off." I wanted to finish the conversation she'd avoided at Bayside.

"He hated it here." She told me what she'd said before. "Finish your turn so I can take mine."

I took the two shots I'd earned, leaving my ball set up as perfectly as I had at the beginning of the game. Hers followed, nicking my ball to earn her a turn but not hard enough to knock me out of position. We stood together while she decided whether to go through the wicket or send my ball into oblivion. She decided to send me. "That's for Gerald. He knew I love it here. Now he can't sell."

"Why did he want to sell? He was tied enough to Calderwood Cove that he had a gravestone put into the cemetery." I hit my ball toward her and missed.

"A monument, you mean. It's all for show. Just like setting up croquet that he never played." She sent her ball through the wicket and moved toward the middle of the course. I didn't catch up to her again. When she hit her ball through the last

182

two wickets, she avoided hitting the finishing stake. "We can play poison. That will give you a chance."

Poison meant that if her ball hit mine, she'd win, but if mine hit hers, I'd win. It didn't make sense because she could easily have hit the post and ended the game. Was she sending me a message about poison, that we were at a stand-off and she was going to win?

It took two turns each before she struck me with her poison ball. "You won," I said as I put my ball and mallet into the cart.

"I plan on lots more wins. Peter's a good opponent."

"You said you were going to see him later. Did you have something planned?"

"He's just going to give me some ideas for how to renovate the cottage for our artists' retreat. So much better than condos."

"I still don't understand. If Gerald was so proud of the lineage of this house, why was he selling?"

"All I can do is guess. Leo told me Gerald didn't have as much money as people thought. Fortunately for me, there's a big insurance policy."

"Did Gerald owe money?"

"You mean is that why someone murdered him? I don't think so. Selling the property wasn't just about money. Every year he complained about coming here, living with ancient bathrooms and a second rate golf course. He always called Esther a nosy bitch and he hated Nelson. Can't say I blame him. Nelson always looks at me like he's undressing me."

"I noticed that," I said. "Does he frighten you?"

"No. He's old and impotent. I imagine."

"So Gerald was going to give up all the Calderwood history and sell?"

"Not quite. There was one clause in the sale. The property had to be named Calderwood Estates."

"So he'd still get to announce the Calderwood name."

"Build something all of Calderwood Cove would hate and take away the one place I feel free." She slammed her mallet into the cart and started toward the porch.

I was tempted to take out another mallet as a weapon. Was Brenda lying? Did she know about the sale and kill Gerald so she'd own the property? She was moving awfully fast in planning her artists' retreat. Before I reached the stairs I saw Nelson's truck pulling into his driveway. Did she use his attraction to her and get him to take Gerald and a tainted oyster to Gerald's boat at dawn on Wednesday?

CHAPTER 20

I STOPPED AT the porch steps and said, "We should ask Nelson about the envelope he gave Gerald.

"What envelope?"

I forgot that Brenda wasn't with me when I told Rachel and Krista about their argument around the croquet set.

"Esther saw Nelson give Gerald some kind of envelope a week ago. Gerald got angry and tore it up. I told the police."

"You can ask him."

I thought for a moment that "him" meant Gerald and that Brenda had lost touch with reality. But her voice was calm when she added, "I'm going inside before the mosquitoes arrive."

"Aren't you interested?"

"Not particularly." She climbed the stairs, leaving me alone. I'd do what she said and ask Nelson. I crossed the street, ready to confront him, to ask him if the envelope involved the oyster fraud, maybe something about fair payment.

Brenda was right about the mosquitoes. I swatted two before I reached the Sprouls' side porch. It felt confining, a stoop more than a long porch like Brenda's. The outside light was on, attracting more mosquitoes.

Esther opened the door before I had a chance to knock. She wore yet another lounging suit, an emerald green one that nearly matched her eyes. "Come inside. It's mosquito time. They'll disappear in an hour or so when the sun finishes setting. If you live in Maine, you learn to live with mosquitoes. Folks around here don't want any spraying. We outsmart them and stay inside at dawn and dusk. They help keep the tourists away."

"Same where I live." I remembered that on Saturday she said something similar about tourists and stormy nights. I stepped into her sitting room where, thankfully, she hadn't turned on the squeaky fan. I slapped a mosquito that followed me inside. Blood spotted my fingers. I could already feel the itch starting.

"Let me get you something for that." Esther disappeared. Moments later, she reappeared carrying a spray bottle of something.

"It's just Benadryl," she said. "I always keep some in my bathroom medicine cabinet. Best thing to stop an itch before it starts."

She sprayed some onto my neck and rubbed it in. She pressed harder than necessary.

Nelson came in from the back door and hung a baseball hat on the coat rack. His hair looked grayer than four days ago and his five o'clock shadow darker. Behind his glasses his green eyes had lost their sharpness. He hadn't been arrested, but the charges against him had taken a toll.

"You look tired. There's chowder on the stove for your dinner." Nelson was sixty years old, but Esther still hovered over him like a smother-mother.

He avoided looking at me. "What's she doing here?"

Esther set the spray bottle of Benadryl on her coffee table next to a blanket she was knitting. "Good question. What are you doing here?"

I spoke directly to Nelson. "I saw your truck come in. When I was playing croquet with Brenda I remembered that your mother told me you gave Gerald an envelope. Brenda deserves to know if it might connect to his murder."

"What are you talking about?"

Esther answered before I could. "I saw you with Gerald a week ago. You handed him an envelope and he tore it up."

"And you told her?" He gestured toward me.

"Only after we heard about Gerald," said Esther. "I thought you might know something that would help catch his killer."

"You should stay out of my business." Nelson stepped toward Esther and she stepped away as if she was afraid of her own son.

I moved closer to her. "What was in the envelope?"

"I suppose you told the police." He addressed me, not Esther.

"I did," I answered. "I'm guessing it involved the oyster fraud. Was he involved?"

"How should I know? My oyster farm might be guilty, but I'm not." He turned from me to Esther. "He was going to sell."

"He? You mean Gerald? Sell what?" Esther spit out her questions.

"Sit down and I'll explain." He motioned Esther to the sofa. When I started to follow, he grabbed my arm. "Not you." The pressure on my arm hurt. I ignored his command and sat next to Esther.

She looked defiant, her green lounge suit matching the vitality of her face. "Hurry up and explain so Deborah can go home and I can go to bed."

"It was an official notification from the zoning board about a hearing for proposed condos. Gerald was selling the property to the guy who built all those condos across from Bayside."

Esther lowered her head. When she lifted it, her eyes glowed. "Why would he do that? Why didn't he tell you? You were friends."

"We weren't friends. We had strictly a business arrangement. He didn't like me."

I reached for Esther's hand. "Brenda only learned about this on Monday when she saw Gerald's lawyer. She thinks he was selling to spite all the people in Calderwood Cove."

"You mean us?" Esther's voice was so low I could barely hear what she said.

Nelson hovered over us, his face contorted, his hands clenched into a fist. "Everyone. Apparently Gerald hated the house but liked his reputation. The sale has a clause that says the condos will be called Calderwood Estates."

"Can't you stop him?" Esther seemed confused as she appealed to Nelson.

"He's dead. I don't know if the sale is final."

"It's not," I said. "Brenda owns the property. She's going to turn the cottage into a rental unit for artists."

Nelson gasped. "What the hell's next. I suppose she's been talking to Peter MacDonald about it. Calderwood Cove used to be a place for boat builders and oyster farmers and lobster fishermen. Now we just get rich summer people from Boston and hippie artists or drug addicts like that O'Donnell kid."

"You know who he is?" I said.

"Of course. He's been haunting me ever since Maureen and Leroy disappeared. Seems to think he can take their place. I just paid him off and should be rid of him for good."

"Their place for what?" I said.

He didn't answer. Instead he went to the window and looked out at the sheriff's car that had just stopped in front of the house. "Now what? I've told them all I know."

I felt like I'd been watching a scene in a movie. A broken woman. A defiant son. An undercurrent of something unsaid beneath Nelson's comment that Gerry couldn't "take their place." He didn't move so I got up to open the door. Holland and Abu stood under the porch light encased in the fog that had rolled in.

Abu took a piece of paper out of his pocket. "Nelson Sproul, we're arresting you on a charge of tax evasion and selling oysters illegally." He began to read him his Miranda rights.

Nelson obeyed the Miranda caution by keeping a defiant silence. It was Esther who found the energy to defy the charge. She jumped from the sofa and began pounding on Abu's chest. I pulled her away.

Holland touched her shoulder. "I'm sorry, Esther. We found Maureen and Leroy O'Donnell. They confessed everything."

Esther pushed his hand away. "They're liars. They have no proof."

"I'm afraid they do," said Holland. "We found the mini-safe I saw Leroy buying two weeks ago. It had over $50,000 in it and an account book with Nelson's signature. Leroy and Maureen owed Nelson half of that money. That was only for June. A lot more money is involved. There's no question that he's guilty."

Esther looked at Nelson then faced Holland. "How could he give them thousands of oysters to sell? He doesn't even go out on the boats."

Abu stopped Holland from answering and addressed Nelson. "Want to tell us who else was involved? Here or at the station?"

Nelson remained silent.

"Ask the O'Donnell's son," I said. "I saw Nelson give him an envelope yesterday. I told Abu that on the phone."

Nelson broke his silence. "You nosy bitch." He turned to Holland. "You can arrest that drug addict for blackmail. Arrest them all for killing Gerald Calderwood. At least he didn't ask for money. All he wanted was a free account for all the oysters his club in Boston ordered."

"The Algonquin Club," I said to Abu and Holland. "It's prestigious enough they could pay for their oysters."

"Prestigious or not, they were freeloading," Nelson said. "Just like all rich people. Maybe the O'Donnells didn't murder Gerald. Check out his rich business friends in Boston. I didn't murder him."

"We're charging you with fraud, not murder." Holland turned from Nelson to Esther. "We're taking Nelson now. Unless he's labeled a flight risk, which I doubt, he'll get released in the morning along with a court date. You'll be able to see him."

Abu opened the door and they led Nelson outside.

Esther collapsed onto the sofa. A tear found a wrinkle on her cheek. She wiped it away. A second tear found the other cheek. I let her cry while I went to her bathroom. A box of tissues sat on the back of the toilet inside a ceramic holder painted with a design of various sized oysters. Above the toilet hung a painting of oyster cages. On the wall across from the toilet, a wooden sign read Sproul's Oyster Farm. It was so weathered I could just make out a date beneath the letters. 1977. Not nearly as old as Esther's nineteenth-century house. Oyster farming came much later to Maine. It didn't matter. The oyster theme was as strong as Gerald's Calderwood crest theme except that it permeated only the bathroom. I left the bathroom carrying the box of tissues I took out of the holder.

When I came back into the sitting room, Esther had taken off her glasses and her hair had fallen out of its bun. She was pushing it away from her eyes. I sat next to her and held out the box of tissues. I took off her glasses and cleaned them. With her flyaway hair, she looked cadaverous. She used a half dozen tissues before she finished, stuffing each of them into the pocket of her lounge pants. If she forgot to take them out before she washed the pants, she'd have a paper wad as big as an oyster shell. I cringed at my metaphor.

I gave her back her glasses. "Let me help you." I found the band that held her hair in place and cinched it into a ponytail.

She put her glasses on, sighed deeply, and said, "I knew something was wrong."

"Is that why you wanted to see what was in his computer?"

She nodded. "I wanted to see how much trouble the farm is in. He needs to sell it before the climate changes so much that no one can raise oysters. No one will buy it. He must have been trying to get enough money to live on if the farm collapses."

I thought of the oyster design in the bathroom. "Would he lose this house? He seems proud of it."

"Only if I die." She spoke as if she were fifty instead of ninety and told me what I already knew. "The house belonged to my family. The Bristols. He owns the one in Damariscotta that belonged to the Sprouls. When my husband died, Nelson only inherited the Sproul house."

"So if he's convicted, you won't lose this one."

"What difference does it make? I'll lose my son." She started to cry again. "He's a good man. Gerald must have talked him into the fraud."

"Nelson said Gerald only wanted free oysters for The Algonquin Club."

"Doesn't mean it wasn't his idea to begin with." She threw down the box of tissues and stood up. "Nelson hated Gerald. So did I. But neither of us killed him."

She started toward the stairs, leaving me to wonder why she denied something I hadn't accused her of. I waited, listening to her reach the top of the stairs. The wind had picked up outside and the whole house rattled. If Nelson was convicted of fraud and lost the house in Damariscotta, Esther might have to spend winters alone in Calderwood Cove. Unless he was convicted of murder as well as fraud, Nelson would be out of jail in a few years. I thought of the irony if Esther had to sell her property and buy a condo for herself in Damariscotta.

The toilet flushed upstairs. I waited longer, listening to the creaks of the old house. The door to Peter's apartment slammed. I went to the window to see if he was crossing the street to meet with Brenda. The light at Brenda's back door illuminated his tall body. She came outside and they went together into the cottage she planned to turn into an artists' retreat.

It was time for me to go back to Brenda's. I'd leave in the morning, forget about Calderwood Cove and oyster frauds and murder. I went to the door then changed my mind. I should check on Esther. She was an old woman who would have to bear the loss of a son she loved.

I crept up the stairway. A night light cast a faint glow into the hallway. Esther's door was open. Her clothes draped over a chair looked like some beast ready to pounce. Under her quilt, I could just make out the shape of her body curled in a fetal position. Her hair covered her face until she lifted her head and opened her eyes to look at me then closed them, her head dropping onto the pillow into a still life of sleep.

CHAPTER 21

THE FOG WASN'T as thick as last night when I'd found the back door locked and had to inch my way to the front porch. Tonight it felt more humid than cold, though I still could have used a sweater over the Town of Shelby T-shirt I was wearing. The light in the cottage cast a glow over the walkway. I could see Brenda and Peter sitting close to each other on a sofa, a bottle of wine on the coffee table in front of them. I brushed away a thought that they were lovers. They weren't touching and I could see Peter writing in a notebook.

I knocked on the door. They'd want to know about Nelson. Brenda opened it. Backlit, she looked like an ad for the artists' retreat they planned. The light accented the reddish tone of her hair that curled along her shoulders. She wore a collarless linen blouse whose brown accented her eyes. "Come in and tell us what the police wanted," she said.

Peter stayed on the sofa while I told them about Nelson's arrest. "Did he kill Gerald?" He set his notebook on the table. It was filled with figures.

"They're not accusing him of that. Nelson learned about Gerald's plan to sell this house but that had nothing to do with the oyster fraud. Nelson was trying to sell Sproul's Oyster Farm before global warming changes the climate so much there'll be no oyster farming in Maine. Esther's more worried about Nelson going to jail than she is about a condo development."

"What will happen to him?" Brenda sat down, leaving me standing near the door.

"I'm not clear on the legal process, but it sounds like they'll charge him and set a court date. They said he'll be able to come back to Calderwood Cove tomorrow."

Brenda reached for her wine, the tremor in her hand showing her nerves. "What if he's lying? What if he killed Gerald? Will I be safe?"

Peter took her glass away and steadied her hand. "There's no reason to kill anyone else. We'll be fine."

Brenda pulled her hand away and picked up her wine glass again, controlling the tremor the way she did when she painted. I wondered if it would eventually get so bad she'd no longer be able to steady it. What would it be like to rent an artist's studio if she had to stop painting? "What about Esther? Will she sell the house, leave the Cove?" she said.

"Nelson owns the house in Damariscotta. If he gets a big fine, he'll lose that, but Esther owns this one. It belonged to her family, the Bristols. It will be hard if she has to live in it all winter alone."

Peter looked at me. "We know that. The apartment I'm in is huge and there's also a cottage. It's a perfect property to house more artists."

Brenda swallowed some wine. "I'm not ready to think about that."

"We'll talk about it later, then," said Peter, as if he were in charge.

I backed toward the door. The idea of creating an artists' retreat was a good one, but they were moving so fast they frightened me. "I'll say goodbye to you now, Peter. I'm leaving in the morning."

He got up from the sofa and gave me a quick hug. "I'm glad you were here. Don't worry about Brenda. I'll look out for her."

"Thank you," I said. I left the cottage and walked quickly to the main house. A car crept past, its headlights casting an eerie glow into the fog. Nothing else stirred. I opened the door into the dining room, using its light to find my way. The clock loomed in front of the stairway, a shadowy presence that suddenly began its chiming. I jumped as if it had attacked me. Ten chimes. Not late, but I felt like I'd been up for days.

I found the switch for the light. It didn't turn on. I held the railing as I climbed to the upstairs hallway. The only light came from the bathroom whose window let in a sliver from the cottage. I found the switch at the top of the stairs but the hall light stayed dark. Brenda would have to change the bulb. Or ask Peter to change it. I suspected that he'd take the place of Leroy as her handyman. I felt my way along the hallway to my room and switched on the nightstand light. Outside the window, the enormous shape of Esther's house inhabited the fog like one of the ships that used to be built there.

A small sailboat was pursuing a white whale. The whale breached, releasing a plume of vapor above its blowhole. The boat crashed against the rocks and startled me out of my dream. I felt like the bed was rolling in a turbulent sea and that my bladder was about to burst into its own vaporous stream. My door was open and the hallway was dark. I reached for my cell phone on the nightstand, turned on its light, and got out of bed.

I came into the hallway and looked into Brenda's studio. The single bed was empty. The door to the room Rachel had used was open and the one to Krista's was closed. Brenda must have claimed Krista's for herself. The light from my phone was enough for me to see in the bathroom. I set it on the floor, used the toilet, and washed my hands.

When I bent to pick up my phone, I saw the beam of a headlamp and someone lurking around the cottage. The tall, thin shape that even without my glasses I could tell was Gerry's. He tried the door. When it didn't open, he went to a shape that looked like a bicycle that was leaning against the cottage. He grabbed something and went to a window. I watched him pull off the screen, push up the window, throw a mound that must be a sleeping bag inside. He boosted himself through the window. Peter told me he'd been in the cottage before. I wondered if he'd been using it to sleep in ever since Maureen and Leroy left.

I stopped in front of Brenda's door then changed my mind. I'd call Abu before I woke her.

I turned on the light in my bedroom, found my glasses, and punched in his number.

"Bashiir Abu," he answered, his voice groggy with sleep.

"It's Deborah Strong," I said.

"I see that. What's so urgent that you're calling me at midnight."

"It's Gerry O'Donnell. He broke into Brenda Calderwood's cottage. I think he's been sleeping there."

"I'll call it right in. The Damariscotta police can get there much faster than I can."

He hung up, leaving me to realize that I was freezing. I took my bathrobe and a pair of socks out of my suitcase. Downstairs, the grandfather clock sounded one note. Abu was wrong. I'd woken him after midnight.

I turned my cell phone light on, went to the room Brenda was in, and opened the door. She was sleeping on her back, her quilt pulled up to her chin, her hair spread against her pillow. She slept in the same position she used to when we had sleepovers in high school. Her face was relaxed, peaceful. I shook her gently. She sat up, startled. "What are you doing? It's the middle of the night."

"Gerry O'Donnell just broke into your cottage. I called the police."

"Who's he?"

"The red-haired man who's been hanging around with his bicycle." If Gerry was her son, Brenda didn't seem to know it.

"Why would he do that?"

"It looks like he's been using it for a place to sleep."

She pulled herself out of bed. "I wish I had a gun."

"We won't need one. He threw a sleeping bag through the window. He's probably sleeping now."

She stumbled into the hallway. "Damn light. It's burned out."

I held her arm so we could descend the stairs together using my phone for light. She flicked the switch in the living room. I followed her into the kitchen where she took two remaining knives out of the holder. "Just in case," she said.

We opened the back door to the cold of the night. A raccoon sniffed around Gerry's bicycle then ambled into the road and headed toward the Beach Club. Nothing stirred in the cottage.

"See if you can find one of Gerald's sweaters," she said. "I'm freezing."

While she waited inside at the open door, I walked through the living room. Dark spots marked the nail holes where Gerald's photos and paintings had hung. I went through the smaller sitting room to the bedroom Brenda had shared with Gerald. His clothes were still strewn across the bed. I fumbled among them until I found a cardigan with only a single slash on the sleeve.

I paused when I came back into the sitting room. *Wuthering Heights* lay closed on the table. Brenda's painting of the barn still hung over the sofa. The cow seemed to be looking at the novel, judging the detritus of ill-conceived marriages. I tied my robe tighter and went back through the main living room into the dining room just as a dark blue police cruiser from Damariscotta pulled into the parking area. Whoever was driving left the car running, its headlights pointed through the fog to the cottage. "You go," said Brenda. "I'll watch from here."

When I stepped outside, I realized I wasn't wearing shoes. I ignored the dampness seeping through the socks and onto my feet.

Scotty Holland got out of the driver's seat and asked, "Where's Brenda?"

A smaller officer got out of the passenger side. "You'll freeze out here," he said, looking at my shoeless feet.

"I'll be okay. Brenda's at the door."

"I see her now," said Holland. "We'll get this Gerry character out of here and she can decide if she wants to press charges."

The two officers went to the door, knocked, and announced themselves. When there was no answer, they called in unison. "We're coming in."

The smaller officer took out a tool and unlocked the door.

"You stay here," Holland said to me.

I didn't have long to wait. The smaller officer came out first, rolling up Gerry's sleeping bag. Holland followed with Gerry, his hands cuffed behind his back. He stopped to check that the door locked when he closed it. "Window's also locked," he said to me. "We'll send someone in the morning to put the screen back in."

Gerry resisted moving when he reached his bike. "I wasn't doin' nothin'. Just findin' a warm place to sleep."

"It's called trespassing," said Holland. "Not such a good idea when someone from this property has been murdered."

"Whatever. I can sleep in a jail cell just as well. But I need my bike."

"We'll get it in the morning," said Holland.

The smaller officer picked up the bike. "We'll put it in the trunk." He looked at Holland. "There's been a fraud and a murder. Forensics will check the bike."

"I had nothin' to do with those." Gerry kicked at the car tire.

"Then you'll be cleared," said the officer as he put the bicycle into the trunk. It only half-closed, so he found a rope in the trunk and secured it.

Holland pushed Gerry into the back seat of the car. Before he closed the door, Gerry yelled at me. "Bitch. You should have been sleepin' like every other night I used this cottage."

Holland closed the door on him then went to speak with Brenda. When he came back, he spoke to his partner. "She'll think about pressing charges. We'll come back in the morning." He turned to me. "Go to bed now. Nothing else will happen tonight." He and the second officer got into the cruiser and drove away.

I went into the house. Brenda handed me one of the knives. "Keep this by your bed."

I took the knife and repeated what Holland had said. "Nothing else will happen tonight." I hoped it was true.

CHAPTER 22

RIBBONS OF SUNRISE were casting a pink glow into my room when I woke up. I rolled out of bed and went to the window. The fog had lifted, leaving enough moisture in the air to intensify the colors. Tones of red rose over the horizon. "Red sky in the morning, sailors take warning." A foolish saying. This sunrise promised spectacular weather. Never mind the lupine and "How Great Thou Art," Calderwood Beach Club would host Gerald's funeral on a day he could have ordered himself. I should stay with Brenda until it was over, but I preferred not to.

The squeak of Peter's Volkswagen coming out of Esther's parking area joined the squawk of seagulls welcoming the dawn. I moved to the side window and watched it pass. Peter would support Brenda. They'd plan the artists' retreat together. She didn't need me.

I could see the light in Esther's kitchen. She was up early waiting for Nelson to be returned. He'd have time enough before any trial to prepare his mother for her future. I imagined her with Brenda and Peter running the retreat center. It would be good for her. She'd have people around who would appreciate her pies. She didn't need me now any more than Brenda needed me. I could come back in a couple of weeks when the reality of death and prison set in.

I found my lightweight pants and a T-shirt in my suitcase, ignoring the blueberry stain on the hem of the shirt I'd worn when we picked. I'd hide it with my sweater until the air warmed. Bath towel, hand towel, facecloth all hung rumpled on the wooden towel rack. I wasn't like the woman in *Sleeping with the Enemy* lining up their edges. I wondered if Gerald used to check on the upstairs rooms, if he aligned the towels, or if he monitored Maureen's cleaning.

I added towels and facecloth to the clothes I was carrying and went into the hallway. Brenda's studio was empty and the door to the room that had been Krista's was still open. She was lying in the same position she'd been in last night. Daylight revealed the towel rack I hadn't seen then. In place of the white towels was a set of blue ones designed with birds in various shades of white and darker blues. The edges of the towels were lined up perfectly, a tag dangling from the bath towel. I recognized the design from ones I'd seen in Renys. Brenda rolled onto her side. "Good morning," I said at the door, checking if she was awake.

She sat up. With her hair uncombed and her face groggy from sleep, she looked like a madwoman in the attic, more *Jane Eyre* than *Wuthering Heights*. "Close the door," she said and lay back down.

I went downstairs to start the coffee and to shower. The nail holes seemed to follow me like the eyes of the barn's cow. Nothing felt safe. When I turned on the shower, I shook off the image of Janet Leigh in the *Psycho* shower scene. It was silly. Wherever Gerald had been murdered, it wasn't in this house.

I finished dressing and opened the bathroom door, surprised by Brenda who was standing in front of it clutching the blue towels to her chest. She wore the thin silk nightgown she'd had on last night. The clothes she held included the sweater she'd worn to Monhegan Island, not Gerald's cardigan.

"I got up to tell you not to leave yet," she said. "Have breakfast with me."

"I started the coffee. I'll wait until you're dressed to have mine." I thought of the blueberries we'd picked that were in the refrigerator and hadn't gone into Esther's scones. "I can make us blueberry pancakes if you have milk and eggs and flour."

"There should be plenty. Maureen stocked up before you came. There's maple syrup from Parker's Maple Barn. You remember it. Right next to Shelby."

"Of course. I still go to Parker's. Why do you have maple syrup from there instead of from Maine?"

"Mail order. Gerald actually listened to me when I asked for it. My nod to the past. Remember when I got my driver's license and I drove all of us for breakfast?" Brenda started on the "when" memories she'd been falling into all weekend.

"Breakfast at noon as I remember." I'd had enough of the past. And the present. I wanted to go home and let her future unfold as it would. "Take your shower and I'll make the pancakes. It's a beautiful morning. We can eat on the porch, then I'll have to leave."

"I wish you'd stay. It's going to be a long day," she said as she closed the bathroom door behind her.

I went upstairs, hung the towels on the rack, straightening the edges so they were even. Gerald's obsessions had infected the air.

Brenda forked her last bite of pancake just as a Damariscotta cruiser pulled up to Esther's house. The officer from last night got out of the front seat. Nelson got out of the back, said something, and abruptly went into the house.

The officer saw us on the porch and crossed the street. He climbed the steps and spoke to Brenda as he nodded toward me.

"Did she tell you about Nelson?"

Brenda looked up at him. "Never mind him. Is this Gerry person still in jail?"

I wondered again about the name, wondered if she knew more than she was admitting.

"He is." The officer's name tag identified him as E. Francoeur. "You'll need to press charges or we'll have to release him." His accent told me that French was his first language and that he was likely a descendant of one of the French Canadians who came to Maine in the nineteenth century looking for jobs in the timber and mill industries.

"How do I do that?" She pushed away her plate.

"Come into Damariscotta, talk to Gerry O'Donnell, and then decide."

"Never mind. I've got a funeral to go to. Get him into an apartment somewhere. I'll pay."

Francoeur looked surprised. "That's very generous. Do you know this man?"

"Just what Deborah told me about him. Make the apartment conditional on drug rehab. I inherited my husband's estate. I have money."

"If you're sure," said Francoeur.

"I'm sure." Brenda picked up her plate and went inside.

I walked Francoeur to the cruiser across the street. "What will happen to Nelson?"

"He doesn't want a jury trial. He'll go before a judge and plead guilty. He says he was cheating so he could pay his employees and keep the business running. It's tough in Maine these days."

"He'll plead guilty to fraud?"

"Correct. Fraud only." I thought he murmured "for now" under his breath as he got into the cruiser and drove away.

I went onto Esther's stoop and rang the bell so I could say

goodbye. She answered the door and stepped outside. She looked the same as she had when I first met her. The same bright pink lounge suit, hair fixed neatly in a bun, the wrinkles and curved body of an old woman. It took me a moment before I saw what was different. Her glasses. A crack ran horizontally across the top of the lens.

"You broke your glasses," I said.

She motioned me inside. Nelson was sitting at the dining room table facing me. He mouthed something then bent his head to sip from a coffee mug. Esther took off her glasses and studied them. "Nelson hugged me so hard when he got home, they fell off. I didn't notice this crack." She ran her bony finger across the lens. Without glasses to hide her green eyes, I saw how beautiful she must once have been. She put the glasses on and became again an old woman.

"Come sit down and have some tea," she said.

"I just came to say goodbye. I'm going home to Shelby."

"Won't you stay for Gerald's funeral?"

"We have a program scheduled at the library tonight so I really need to get back."

"What kind of program's so important?"

The program was on gravestones. I dodged the question so I wouldn't have to bring up more death. "It's a program sponsored by the New Hampshire Humanities Council. The presenter is an historian from UNH and a good friend of mine. I'll come back in a couple of weeks when I might be useful."

"I'll miss you, but Nelson will come with Brenda and me."

Nelson had been listening. "I'm not going," he yelled from the kitchen table. "I'm getting ready for jail."

"You'll come with me." Esther yelled back at him as if he were a five-year-old, then said to me, "That nice policeman said he'll probably lose the oyster farm, but he might not go to jail." She stepped forward to hug me. The edge of her glasses clinked my temple.

I pulled away and took both her hands in mine. "I'm sorry for all this."

"Don't be sorry for Brenda. We'll all be happier without Gerald strutting around like King Calderwood." She pressed her fingernails hard into my hands.

"Goodbye then," I said as I backed out the door. I looked at my hand. Her fingernails were sharp. A drop of blood colored the space between my thumb and finger.

Esther followed me outside in time to see Peter's Volkswagen come fast on the road that curved just before her house and Brenda's. "He drives too fast," she said. "But he's a good tenant. And friend."

We watched him pull into Brenda's parking area. He got out of the car, took a cooler from the backseat, and tried the door to the cottage. It was still locked. Brenda must have heard his car because she came out of the house and unlocked the door. They went into the cottage.

Esther ran her hand along the front of her lounge suit. "Peter told me before he left this morning that they plan to turn that cottage into an artists' retreat. It will be good for Brenda. Life begins at widowhood."

I was surprised to hear Esther say the same thing Peter had said. She'd never spoken about her husband. I only knew about their relationship because of Peter. "It didn't for me," I said.

"I'm sorry for you then." She gave me a quick hug and went inside to the looming house.

I crossed the street to say a last goodbye to Brenda and Peter. Peter opened the cottage door when I knocked. I could see Brenda in the kitchenette looking through the notebook she and Peter were using last night. She motioned me over. There were only two chairs at the table, so Peter stood at the counter while I sat. The chair creaked. It matched the pine table and both needed repair. I wondered if furniture would come with the cottage renovations.

She read my thoughts the way she did when we were kids. "Look at our plans." She slid the notebook to me. A sketch showed an interior where the walls separating the kitchen and the living room were removed. Instead of the table, there was a bar with two stools between the kitchen and the living room. The sofa was replaced with two upholstered chairs, a coffee table between them. The wall across from them had floor to ceiling bookcases. The front window was enlarged. An easel and a table with paints faced outwards. Brenda had sketched lines to represent sun streaming from a skylight. The studio would have a view only of the main house, but it would have plenty of light.

She took the book from me and turned the page. "Peter wants a desk. I told him this studio is for a painter, not a poet. He insisted so we'll put it in the bedroom."

The sketch of the bedroom showed a single bed, a nightstand, and a minimalist desk placed in front of a side window. The front window had a sill filled with houseplants. I turned the page to a last sketch. The bathroom with a clawfoot tub. The one picture Brenda had sketched in her drawings hung on the wall beside the tub. It was her painting of the barn with the cow's head.

"Why this painting in the bathroom?" I said.

"I drew it when I was telling Peter about Joseph Wheeler. It won't hang in here. I'll keep it where it is in my sitting room." She handed the book to me. "Don't leave yet. I want to show you the logo I created this morning. I'm calling the retreat Painting at Peterson's. My name, not Calderwood. I'll be right back. It's in the house."

"Brenda's a great designer," Peter said as she left the cottage. "I was calculating the cost when you came in last night." He bent over me and turned the page to a long list of items and figures. "I'll have more than enough money for all of this."

His pronoun registered. "Don't you mean Brenda will have enough money?"

"I meant to say 'Brenda and I.'"

"Is she including you in a partnership? She's calling the center Painting at Peterson's."

He leaned against the counter, his face taut and his fists clenched. I pushed my chair back and faced him. One brown eye from Brenda. One blue from Gerald. I pulled the name out of my memory of that long ago biology class where we'd talked about eyes. Heterochromia.

Pieces locked into place. Peter cultivating a friendship when he was a valet at The Algonquin Club. His claim to be a poet but with no poems to show anyone. His visit to the lawyer with Brenda. His conversation with me when we drove to get lobsters and him saying to put them in a pot and watch them die. Brenda had named her baby Peter, not Gerald. Did he know the man he'd called a bastard was his father?

I backed away from him. "Did you or Brenda have the idea of the retreat center?"

"It's a sweet idea."

"Whose idea?"

"Doesn't matter. It'll make me good money. I never had much growing up. Not like Brenda."

"Does Brenda know?"

"Know what?"

"That you're her son."

"Why do you say that?"

"You've been acting like you're her confidante." I studied his face. "I can see it now. You look like her father. You're a Peterson. When did you find out?"

"It's why I took that job at The Algonquin Club. She'd signed a paper saying her child could find her."

"Was Gerald your father?"

"Record doesn't say. I suppose so. He was a bastard." He used the word again.

"Did you kill him?"

My suspicion turned to fear. He didn't want a partnership with the woman he knew was his mother.

He slid open the top of the cooler. "It doesn't matter. She'll never know that I'm the surviving heir."

He reached into the cooler and came toward me holding something. I knocked over the chair as I backed out of the kitchenette. A rung came out of its hole and the chair lay lopsided on the floor.

"You should have gone home yesterday." He came at me with what he'd taken from the cooler. "Filled with vibrio bacteria. Too much poison in those oysters from Sproul's Oyster Farm. Inspectors will close it. Esther will need money. Her house will be a nice addition to an artists' colony."

He grabbed me before I reached the door, dragged me into the bedroom, and threw me onto the bed. I tried to roll off but he pulled me back and sat on top of me. He cracked open the oyster shell and pushed the oyster against my mouth. I clenched my teeth and lips. He forced them open and shoved the oyster into my mouth. "Fortunately I have a couple of these. Brenda will enjoy a little hors d'oeuvre before Gerald's funeral."

I tried to spit out the oyster but he held my mouth clamped shut. I struggled not to swallow. He pressed his fingers hard against my jaw. My mouth opened a crack. He pried it open and pushed the oyster in further. I gagged as it slid down my throat.

"There's enough bacteria in that oyster to do more than make you sick. It will take a while, but this will help you along." He threw me onto the floor. "I'll tell Brenda the chair broke and you fell. I'll drive slowly when we take you to the hospital."

He lifted my shoulders and smashed my head onto the floor. The last thing I heard was a car door slam.

CHAPTER 23

I WOKE THINKING I was in the infirmary at Murkland College after I'd been attacked last fall. I remembered gagging when someone thrust a tube down my throat. My throat scratched, my head ached, and my stomach felt like I was on a stormy sea. No tubes were attached to my arms so I knew I was okay.

A blurry figure stood at the window. It came closer and I could see that it was Brenda. "What happened?" I managed to say.

She pulled her chair closer to the bed. "Peter killed Gerald."

"I remember that he shoved a contaminated oyster down my throat. The last thing I heard was a car door slam." My voice sounded as bad as I felt.

"Peter heard the car. He came out of the cottage and said you'd fallen. We went inside. You were on the floor and there was an oyster shell next to you."

"We?"

"Scotty Holland and I. Abu stayed outside with Peter. Scotty put you in my car and rushed you here."

"Here?"

"Lincoln Health Hospital in Damariscotta. I had no idea what was going on until I saw Peter in handcuffs."

I managed to keep vomit from rising into my throat and said, "How did they know?"

"They found the mini frig in the boat. It hadn't been destroyed. Peter's fingerprints were on a bottle of Woodford Reserve."

"Gerald's favorite."

"I don't know any details. I just know Peter lured Gerald to the boat and killed him. How did you figure it out?"

"When Peter said 'I'll have enough money for the renovations,' I started to remember some other things he'd said." I struggled again not to gag. "He wasn't going to include you the retreat."

"That doesn't make sense. We were going to be partners. It's still my property, not his."

Brenda hadn't learned that Peter was her son. "Peter was—" I stopped myself. "I don't know. Maybe he thought he would own it because of those papers your lawyer was getting ready. The oyster he fed me was meant for you."

Brenda clutched the blanket on my bed. "The last thing he said when they put him into the sheriff's car was 'I've never written a poem in my life.' How could I be so stupid?"

"You weren't stupid. I never suspected him either."

"I wonder if he had help."

I wondered the same thing. "Did Peter know enough about oysters to lace them with vibrio bacteria?"

"It wouldn't be hard. The water around here is warming enough that he could find a spot to let them sit for a while."

I wished I had my glasses on so I could see Brenda's expression. We'd had to explain about vibriosis to her.

Before I could respond to her, a nurse came into the room and asked, "How's your head?"

"Better than my throat. Can I go home now?"

She took out one of those little flashlights nurses use and had me follow the beam. "Open," she said so she could look in my throat. "We had to pump your stomach. You're lucky they found that oyster shell. Vibrio bacteria can kill."

"We know that." Brenda and I spoke at the same time.

"You can leave the hospital, but no driving until tomorrow. Brenda, wake her a couple of times in the night. She's been sedated and she had a slight concussion. If she's fine in the morning, she can go home."

The nurse left the room that surrounded me in an impressionist blur. "They took my contact lenses. What time is it?"

Brenda looked at the clock. "Just before one. Get yourself dressed. If you feel okay at five o'clock, you'll be coming to Gerald's funeral with me."

I listened as the crowd of people sang the last hymn, "How Great Thou Art," to music coming from an electronic keyboard. I adjusted the glasses I had to wear because I'd run out of contact lenses. The musician looked like a high school kid recruited from his rock band, but he played the hymns well. Beside me, Brenda sang with only a touch of sarcasm when she accented the word "great." On my other side, Esther's voice told me she'd never sung in the church choir. A photo of Gerald and a coal black urn was flanked with the lupine he hated.

It had been a long funeral, one of those where mourners are invited to say a word about the deceased. Men had spoken mostly about Gerald on the golf course or in his sailboat. They shared jokes about his pride in the Calderwood name and his love of oysters on the half shell. As much as rumors had spread about his murder, the vibrio poisoning had remained a secret. The women spoke about Gerald's kind blue eyes and his generosity. The last to speak—the New Jersey woman who'd quizzed me when I walked to the Club yesterday—left us with the hope that Peter MacDonald would get the death penalty. I was surprised at her viciousness.

The moment the hymn ended, people dispersed to a table set out with food. I wondered if the news of Peter's arrest included his attack on me and if everyone was looking at me and the bruise I'd tried to hide on my forehead.

New Jersey's husband, the tennis player, moved to where Brenda, Esther, and I were standing. He gestured to his wife, who was in line at the food table. "She liked Gerald. We're all sorry for your loss, Brenda." He spoke the platitude I'd been hearing since we arrived at the Club. He looked at Esther. "Where's Nelson?"

"Home." Esther hadn't been able to force him into coming to the funeral. She fiddled with the wide belt that cinched her waist. The style was out of date, the belt making her waist look as small as a child's. The dress's green flower print brought out the green of her eyes in the same way her lounge suit had done last night. She fixed those eyes on the tennis man. "You don't need to pretend, Rob. Nelson was selling oysters illegally and avoiding taxes. Wouldn't surprise me if the Beach Club bought a lot of them."

"We only buy legal ones. How was this Peter fellow involved?" He was trolling for information.

Brenda offered as much as she knew. "Gerald planned to sell our Calderwood house. Peter found out before I did. He wanted to stop him. He was going to help me turn our cottage into an artists' retreat."

"So he killed him? That's pretty extreme," said Rob.

"That's the only motive I can think of." If Brenda was telling the truth, she knew nothing about Peter's identity.

Rob sounded shocked when he said, "He was going to sell? Gerald loved being King of Calderwood."

"He hated the Cove," said Brenda. "Actually, he hated all of you."

"Don't tell my wife that." Rob looked toward the food table where his wife had finished loading a plate.

"It doesn't matter." Brenda's tremor began to shake the funeral program. "I own the house now. I'll be turning that cottage into an artists' retreat without the help of Peter. It will be for painters, not poets."

"Why did he get involved?" said Rob. "Was it his idea?"

Esther surprised me when she said, "Actually it was mine. We were just making small talk about both our properties. An artists' retreat would be eligible for grant money. He must have learned that Gerald planned to sell and killed him to stop a sale. He was entitled—" She stopped herself and changed her phrasing. "He loved using my place to write poetry. I'm hoping Brenda will let me be part of this artists' retreat."

Brenda slipped her arm around Esther's cinched waist. "He was lying about writing poetry. But we can still turn our places into a retreat for painters. We'll make a good team. I've already done the designs for the cottage."

"So we'll have more strangers in the Cove. I hope none of them will be murderers." Rob left us for the food table.

"We should eat as well," said Brenda. "After all, I paid for the food."

Esther looked up at me from where she was weeding her garden. She saw the car keys I was holding. "You're leaving?"

"I am. I've said my goodbye to Brenda and wanted to say one to you as well."

She stood up and picked a couple of peas. "Best picked early in the morning. Try these."

"You know," I said as I took the peas.

"Know what?"

"About Peter."

"Why do you think I know something?"

"Yesterday. You said he was entitled. I assume you meant to the inheritance."

"The couple who adopted him divorced. He told me the man was as bad as Gerald. I think he didn't like seeing his mother—Brenda—being treated the same way. How did you know?" She picked a pea and chewed on it.

"It came out yesterday. That's why he attacked me."

"Did you tell Brenda?" she said as she picked another pea.

"No," I said. "She knows Peter was going to poison her with tainted oysters the way he'd poisoned Gerald. She doesn't need to know he's her son. If it comes out later, she'll be in a better state to handle learning that her son killed his own father."

"If Gerald was his father."

"Brenda told us that that he was when she told us about her pregnancy. He didn't want kids. I'm not sure she did either, but her parents convinced her not to have an abortion. How long have you known?"

"Since the beginning. I won't tell her. In case you're wondering, Gerald's murder had nothing to do with the fraud at Sproul's Oyster Farm. Nothing to do with the canceled reservation at Palmetto Dunes."

"You knew what golf resort Gerald was going to?"

"Peter knew."

Peter must have shared confidences with Esther over their cribbage games. She should have shared some of this information. I didn't press her and asked instead, "Why did you want to search Nelson's computer?"

"I knew Nelson wasn't involved in the murder. I told you before. He was worried about money. If Peter and Brenda opened a retreat center, I could join them. It would be income Nelson could use."

I squeezed the peas she'd given me. She'd planned the retreat center from the beginning. She would know how to infect oysters with vibrio bacteria.

She took off her gardening hat and chewed slowly on another pea. "I won't tell Brenda about Peter. He shouldn't have tried to kill her, but all's well that ends well. Even without him, she'll be a good partner." She fixed her green eyes on me. They looked triumphant. A faint smile curled on her lips.

She'd been a perfect performer, a best supporting actress. Without saying goodbye, I dropped the peas in front of her, stepped over the fallen limb that hadn't been removed, and walked away from Calderwood Cove. Time enough to decide if I should let the case be closed and leave Brenda to a brighter future.

ACKNOWLEDGMENTS

*C*ALDERWOOD *COVE* DRAWS on memories of many reunions I've had in Maine with my college roommates. I thank them and their spouses for the way we've stayed connected: Bobbee and Leo, Dolly and Craig, Janet, Linda, Lorraine and Paul, and my husband, Ron. Sadly, Leo and Ron have died, but their memory lives in our gatherings together. Special thanks to Janet, who gave me valuable tips on Damariscotta. Although the setting is based on a real place, none of my friends are models for the characters in my novel.

Thanks go to Alan Thompson who read the full manuscript before I submitted it. Carole Beers, Clive Rosengren, Jenn Ashton, and Michael Niemann keep me writing even through difficult times. Monday Mayhem is an apt name for this critique group. Eddie Vincent, Cynthia Brackett-Vincent, and Deirdre Wait of Encircle Publications have been invaluable for my career. The Encircle Happy Hour group have come to feel like old friends. And thank you to Chris Wait of High Pines Creative for another wonderful cover design.

As ever, I am grateful to my family who keep me moving on.

ABOUT THE AUTHOR

SHARON L. DEAN grew up in Massachusetts where she was immersed in the literature of New England. She earned undergraduate and graduate degrees at the University of New Hampshire, a state she lived and taught in before moving to Oregon. Although she has given up writing scholarly books that require footnotes, she incorporates much of her academic research as background in her mysteries, and continues to write and research in the landscape she's still discovering in the Northwest.

Sharon is the author of three Susan Warner Mysteries as well as a literary novel titled *Leaving Freedom*. Her mystery series featuring librarian and reluctant sleuth Deborah Strong includes *The Barn* (Encircle, 2020), *The Wicked Bible* (Encircle, 2020), and now the third in the series, *Calderwood Cove*, has been published by Encircle in 2022. For the latest news, visit sharonldean.com, and follow Sharon L. Dean, Author, on Facebook, and @sharonldean3 on Instagram.

If you enjoyed reading this book,
please consider writing your honest review
and sharing it with other readers.

Many of our Authors are happy to participate in
Book Club and Reader Group discussions.
For more information, contact us at info@encirclepub.com.

Thank you,
Encircle Publications

For news about more exciting new fiction, join us at:

Facebook: www.facebook.com/encirclepub

Instagram: www.instagram.com/encirclepublications

Twitter: twitter.com/encirclepub

Sign up for Encircle Publications newsletter and specials:
eepurl.com/cs8taP

www.ingramcontent.com/pod-product-compliance
Lightning Source LLC
Chambersburg PA
CBHW020627110726
47899CB00002B/684